michael morpurgo

AN EAGLE
IN THE SNOW

A FEIWEL AND FRIENDS BOOK
An imprint of Macmillan Publishing Group, LLC

AN EAGLE IN THE SNOW. Copyright © 2015 by Michael Morpurgo. All rights reserved.
Printed in the United States of America by LSC Communications US, LLC
(Lakeside Classic), Harrisonburg, Virginia. For information, address Feiwel and Friends,
175 Fifth Avenue, New York, N.Y. 10010.

Our books may be purchased in bulk for promotional, educational, or business use.
Please contact your local bookseller or the Macmillan Corporate and Premium Sales
Department at (800) 221-7945 ext. 5442 or by e-mail at
MacmillanSpecialMarkets@macmillan.com.

Library of Congress Cataloging-in-Publication Data is available.

ISBN 978-1-250-10515-8 (hardcover) / ISBN 978-1-250-10516-5 (ebook)

First published in 2015 in Great Britain by HarperCollins Children's Books,
a division of HarperCollinsPublishers Ltd.

First published in the United States of America by Feiwel and Friends,
an imprint of Macmillan Publishing Group, LLC

Book design by Anna Booth
Feiwel and Friends logo designed by Filomena Tuosto

First U.S. Edition—2017

10 9 8 7 6 5 4 3 2 1

mackids.com

This book is dedicated to
Private Henry Tandey VC.

And this is why. Many of my stories have come from the lives of others, from truths, written or remembered, this one perhaps more than any other. Certainly had I not discovered, through Michael Foreman, the extraordinary story of the life and death of Walter Tull, the first black officer to serve in the British Army, I should never have written A Medal for Leroy. *Had I not met an old soldier from the First World War who had been to that war with horses, in the cavalry, I should not have written* War Horse. *Had I not come across, in a museum in Ypres, an official letter from the army to the mother of a soldier at the front in that same war, informing her that her son had been shot at dawn for cowardice, I should never have told my story of* Private Peaceful. *It was a medal commemorating the sinking of the* Lusitania *by torpedo in 1915 with terrible loss of life, over a thousand souls, that compelled me to think of writing the story of a survivor, which I did in* Listen to the Moon.*

I write fiction, but fiction with roots in history, in the people who made our history, who fought and often died in our wars. They were real people who lived and had their being in another time, often living and suffering through great and terrible dangers, facing these with unimaginable courage. My challenge as a story maker has been to imagine that courage, to live out in my mind's eye, so far as I can, how it must have been for them.

So when I was told by Dominic Crossley-Holland, history producer at the BBC, about the extraordinary life and times of Henry Tandey, the most decorated private of the First World War, I wanted to explore why he did what he did. This I have done, not by writing his biography. That had been done already. Rather I wanted to make his life the basis of a fictional story that takes his story beyond his story and tries to explore the nature of courage and the dilemma we might face when we discover that doing the right thing turns out to be the worst thing we have ever done.

Because the life of Henry Tandey is so closely associated with this story, I thought it right to include the history, so far as it is known, of his actual life. This you will find in the afterword at the end of the book.

Michael Morpurgo
February 16, 2015

PART ONE

— ✦ —

THE 11:50 TO LONDON

1

THE TRAIN WAS STILL IN THE STATION, AND I WAS wondering if we'd ever get going. I was with my ma. I was tired. My arm was hurting and itching at the same time, inside the plaster. I remember she was already at her knitting, her knitting needles *tick-tack*ing away, automatically, effortlessly. Whenever she sat down, Ma would always be knitting. Socks for Dad, this time.

"This train's late leaving," Ma said. "Wonder what's up? That clock on the platform says it's well past twelve already. Still, not hardly surprising, I suppose, under the circumstances." Then she said something that surprised me. "If I drop off to sleep, Barney," she told me, "just you keep your eye on that suitcase, d'you hear? All we got in this world is up there in that luggage rack, and I don't want no one pinching it."

I was just thinking that was quite a strange thing to say, because there was no one else in the carriage except the two of us, when the door opened and a man got in, slamming the door behind him. He never said a word to us, hardly even acknowledged we were there, but took off his hat, put it up on the rack beside our suitcase, and then settled himself into the seat opposite. He looked at his watch and opened up his paper, his face disappearing behind it for a while. He had to put it down to blow his nose, which was when he caught me staring at him and nodded.

Everything about him was neat, I noticed that at once, from his highly polished shoes to his trim mustache and his collar and tie. I decided right away that he didn't look like the sort of man who would pinch Ma's suitcase. There was also something about him that I thought I recognized; I had the feeling I might have seen him before. Maybe I hadn't. Maybe it was just because he seemed about the same age as Grandpa, with the same searching look in his eye.

But this stranger was neat, and there was nothing neat

about my grandpa. My grandpa was a scarecrow, with his hair always tousled—what there was of it—his hands and face grimy from delivering his coal, and that was after he had washed. This stranger had clean hands, and clean nails too, as well looked after as the rest of him.

"Hope I pass inspection, son," he said, eyeing me meaningfully.

Ma nudged me and apologized for my rudeness before she turned on me. "How many times have I told you not to stare at people, Barney? Say sorry to the gentleman now."

"Don't you worry, missus," he said. "Boys will be boys. I was one once myself, a while ago now, but I was." Then, after a moment or two, he went on: "S'cuse me, missus, but this is the London train, isn't it? The 11:50, right?"

"Hope so," said Ma, nudging me again because I was still staring. I couldn't help myself. The station master came past our window then, waving his green flag, blowing his whistle, his cheeks puffed out so that his face looked entirely round, like a pink balloon, I thought. Then we were off, the train chuffing itself, wearily, reluctantly, into slow motion.

" 'Bout time," said Ma.

"Do you mind if I let in a bit of air, missus?" the stranger asked. "I like a bit of air."

"Help yourself," Ma told him. "It's free."

He got up, let the window down a couple of notches on the leather strap, and then sat down. He caught my eye again, but this time he smiled at me. So I smiled back.

"Nine, are you?" he asked me.

Ma answered for me. "Ten. He's a little small for his age. But he's growing fast now. He should be too. He eats for England. Don't know where he puts it."

She was talking about me much as Grandpa might talk about the marrows in his allotment, on and on, but with the same pride and joy, so I didn't mind too much.

The train was gathering speed now, getting into its stride, sounding happier. *Diddle-dee da, diddle-dee da, diddle-dee dee, diddle-dee da.* I loved that sound, loved that rhythm. Nothing more was said for some time. The stranger went back to reading his paper, and I looked out of the window at the rows of bombed-out streets we were passing, and I thought of Grandpa's marrows and his allotment shed, which had been blasted to pieces in the same air raid a couple of nights before. I remembered how he had stood there looking down at the crater where once his vegetables had been growing, all in tidy rows, his cabbages and his leeks and his parsnips. Grandpa's allotment was the only thing tidy about him. That allotment had been his life.

"I'll dig it again, Barney," he'd said, his eyes filling with anger, "you see if I won't. We'll have all the carrots and onions and tatties we need. The beggars who done this, I won't let them win." He brushed away the tears with the back of his hand, and they were fierce tears. "You know something, Barney," he went on, "it's funny: all through the last war, in the trenches, I never hated 'em. They were just Fritzis, fighting like we were. But now it's different. They done what they done to Coventry, my place, my city, my people. I hate 'em, and for what they done to my allotment I hate 'em too. They got no right." He took my hand and held it tight. He'd done that often enough before when I was upset. Now it was him that was upset, and I was squeezing his hand, I was doing the comforting.

But when it came to Big Black Jack, there was no comforting him.

All night during the air raid we'd been down in the shelter in Mulberry Road clutching one another, all of us knowing the next bomb might be the one to get us. You tried not to listen for the next one, but you did. With every bomb that fell you tried to believe it was the last one. But it never was. Grandpa had been the rock Ma and I had clung to, his arms firm and strong around us, holding us tight, and singing his songs, his voice hoarse and loud above all the whimpering and the crying and screaming, and louder still when the bombs were coming closer, when the ground was shaking, when the shelter was full of dust.

When at last the all-clear siren sounded and the terror was over and we came up out of the shelter—how many hours we were down there I do not know—we found the world about us a place of rubble and ruin, hot with fires that were still smoldering everywhere. Mulberry Road, what was left of it, was filled with choking acrid smoke that hung like a fog around us and above us. There was no good air to breathe, no sky to see.

Hoping against hope, we made our way home, to our house at the end of the road. But we had no house. We had no home. And it wasn't just our place that was gone. The whole street was unrecognizable, simply not there. Only the lamppost was left, the one outside where our house had been, the one that shone into my window at nighttime. Friends and neighbors were there, a policeman and an air-raid warden, all clambering over the rubble, scrabbling and searching. Ma said she would stay and see if there was anything that could be recovered. She told Grandpa to take me away. She was upset, crying, and I could tell she didn't want me with her. But my train set was in there somewhere, under all the ruins, and my red London bus I'd got for Christmas and all the tin soldiers on my shelf, my special cockleshell too from the beach at Bridlington.

I ran up onto the rubble and started climbing on my hands and knees.

I was going to look. I was going to find them. I had to. But the air-raid warden caught me by the arm, holding me back, and then, despite all my protests, he was carrying me down again to Ma. "My bus," I cried, "my soldiers, my things."

"It's too dangerous, Barney," she said, shaking my shoulders to make me listen. "Just go with Grandpa. Do as you're told, please, Barney. I'll find what I can, I promise."

So Grandpa took me off to his allotment, just to find out if it was all right, he said. But I knew really that it was because Ma didn't want me there around all those crying people. Mrs. McIntyre was sitting on the pavement outside her shop, her stockings in tatters, her legs bleeding. She was staring into space, fingering her rosary beads, her lips moving in silent prayer. Mr. McIntyre was there somewhere but no one could find him.

It wasn't far from the allotment to the field where Grandpa kept Big Black Jack, our old cart horse, and Grandpa's soul mate since Grandma died—mine too, come to that. Big Black Jack was the horse Grandpa worked with and talked to all day and every day as they delivered coal all around the city, and I'd go with him sometimes, after school and at weekends. I couldn't carry the sacks of coal—they were too heavy. My job was to fold the empty sacks for Grandpa and pile them neatly in the back of the cart, and to make sure Big Black Jack always had corn in his sack and water enough to drink. So Big Black Jack and me, we were best mates.

At first, everything seemed just as it should be: the rickety old shed still standing, and the water bucket by the door full of water, the hay net hanging limp and empty. But there was no sign of Big Black Jack.

Then we saw the smashed fence. He'd got free—not surprising, with all that bombing. "He's took off some-where," Grandpa said. "He'll be fine. That horse can look after hisself. He'll be fine. He's done it before. He'll be back. He'll find his way home, always does."

But I knew even as he was saying it that he was just tell-ing himself, hoping it was true, but fearing the worst.

2

IT WAS ONLY MOMENTS LATER THAT WE FOUND Big Black Jack lying there, stretched out on the grass at the edge of the woods. And through the trees we saw the crater now where a bomb had fallen. The trees around had been blasted, burned, and stunted. Big Black Jack lay so still. There didn't seem to be a mark on him. I looked into his wide-open eyes. Grandpa was kneeling by his great head, feeling his neck. "Cold," he said. "He's cold. Poor old boy. Poor old boy." He cried silently, his whole body shaking.

I didn't cry then, but I nearly was now, in the train, as I remembered it all again, the kindness in his eye, how I longed for him to breathe, not to be so still. I felt the tears welling up inside me.

"You all right, son?" said the stranger opposite, leaning forward. Ma answered for me again, and I was relieved she did this time, for there were tears filling my mouth too, and I couldn't have spoken even if I'd wanted to.

"We was bombed out," Ma explained to him. "Bit upset he is."

"And he's busted his arm too," the man said. "How did that happen?"

"Football," Ma told him. "He's mad on his football, aren't you, Barney?"

I nodded. It was all I could do.

"Lost the house," Ma went on. "On Mulberry Road it was. Lost just about everything. Then, so did lots of others I s'pose. But we got lucky. Still here, aren't we?" She put her hand on mine. "Busted arm in't much, when you think . . . So, mustn't grumble, must we? No point, is there? Just thank our lucky stars. We're off to stay with my sister down in Cornwall, by the sea, aren't we, Barney? Mevagissey. Lovely down there. No bombs there neither.

Just sea and sand and sunshine—and lots of fish. We like fish and chips, don't we, Barney? And we like Aunty Mavis, don't we?"

I did, in a way. But I still couldn't speak.

Ma stopped talking for a while, and we sat there, the train rocking and rattling, the smoke flying past the window. The rhythm was changing, faster, faster. *Dee dum, dee dum, dee dummidy dum.*

"They hit the cathedral an all, y'know," Ma said. "Hardly nothing left of it. Lovely old place too. Beautiful that spire, see it for miles around. What they want to go and do that for? That's wicked, that is. Wicked."

"It is," said the stranger. "And I know Mulberry Road as it happens. I grew up there. In a manner of speaking. I seen what they done to it. I was there afterward, after the raid, pulling folk out. Civil Defense, Air-raid Warden. That's what I do," the stranger went on. He seemed to be talking to himself now, thinking out loud, remembering. "Civil Defense, fire watching, firefighting. But you can't fight a firestorm. Inferno it was. I was there. So I didn't do much good, did I?"

That was the moment I realized where I had seen the

stranger before. He was the air-raid warden I had seen up on the rubble, who had carried me down. He looked different out of uniform, without his tin hat. But it was him. I was sure of it. He was looking hard at me then, frowning, almost as if he had recognized me at the same moment.

"'Spect you did your best," Ma said, oblivious, busying herself with her knitting. "All anyone can do, isn't it? Barney's pa, he's away, overseas, in the army. In the Royal Engineers. He's doing his best. Like his grandpa too. He's staying behind in Coventry, says he's going to carry on like before. Coalman, he is, family business. Houses got to be kept warm, he says. Stoves got to be lit, he says. Can't let down his customers. And I says to him: 'There aren't hardly any houses left.' And he says: 'Then we got to build them up again, haven't we?' So he's staying, doing his best, doing what's right, that's what he thinks. And that's what I think too. No one can ask for more. Just do what you think is right, and you can't go far wrong. You just got to do your best. S'what I tell Barney, don't I, dear?"

"Yes, Ma," I said, finding my voice again. And it was true, she was always telling me that. The teachers at school told me much the same thing, just about every day, in fact.

"But sometimes," said the man, speaking slowly and thoughtfully, "the problem is that your best is not enough. Sometimes, what seems right at the time turns out to be wrong." He sat back in his seat then as if he'd had enough of all this talking. Ma obviously hadn't recognized him. I wanted to tell her, but I couldn't, not with him there. He turned away to look out of the window, and for a long time none of us spoke.

I love trains, everything about them, the hissing and the puffing, the rhythm and the rattle and the rocking, the whistling and the whooping, the roar as you burst into a tunnel, into the deep thunderous blackness, and then suddenly, with no warning, you're out again into the bright light of day, the horses galloping off over the fields, the sheep and crows scattering. I love stations too, the bustle of them, the slamming of doors, the guard in his peaked cap, flag waving, and the engine breathing, waiting for the whistle. Then, the whistle at last, and the *chuff, chuff, chuff*ing.

I'd told Dad the last time he was home on leave that I had made up my mind to be a train driver when I grew up. Dad loved tinkering with engines—generators, motorcycles, cars—he could fix anything. So he was pleased I was going to be a train driver, I could tell. He told me the steam engine was just about the most beautiful machine man ever created. Just being in the train that morning was a comfort to me. I may not have been able to put out of my mind the night of terror down in the shelter, nor the dreadful sights we had witnessed the next day— Mrs. McIntyre sitting there on the pavement with her rosary beads, her home and her life in ruins—our house reduced to rubble, and Grandpa kneeling over Big Black Jack. But the rhythm and rocking of the train soothed me somehow, and made me sleepy too.

Beside me, Ma had stopped talking altogether and was fast asleep, her head hanging down loose as if it would fall off at any moment. Her hands were still holding her knitting needles, and her ball of wool lay in her lap. Half a sock for Dad already done.

So that left just me and the stranger opposite—who, it turned out, was not such a stranger after all. He was looking at me from time to time as if he was about to ask me a question, then thought better of it. Finally, he leaned forward, speaking to me under his breath: "It was you I carried down, after the raid, wasn't it, son? In Mulberry Road?"

I nodded.

"Thought so," he said. "Mulberry Road kids, you and me both then. Never forget a face. I remember thinking, as I was carrying you down, that you reminded me of me—at your age, I mean. I had a busted arm once, when I was little. Not football—fell off a bike. Good to meet up again. Spitting image of me, you are." He was smiling at me and nodding. Then he went on: "Your dad, where is he, where's he fighting? Where did the army send him?"

"Africa," I told him. "In the desert. He looks after the tanks, makes them work, mends them when they break. Sand gets into everything, he says. Hot too, he says, millions of flies."

"That's where I should be," the man said. "I was there once, in the army. South Africa, long time ago. S'what I should be doing now, fighting, like your dad. But they wouldn't let me join up. Gammy leg." He was patting his knee. "From the last war. Bit of shrapnel still in there somewhere. And anyway, I'm too old, they said. Forty-five?

Too old? Stuff and nonsense. So I got to sit at home and do nothing. Civil Defense, Air-raid Warden, that's all I'm good for now, going and blowing whistles, telling people to close their curtains in the blackout. I should be out there fighting. I told them—more than anyone I should be out there, doing my bit, like your dad. I ain't too old. I can still run about a bit. I can stand and fight, can't I?" His lips were quivering now. I could see he was struggling to control himself, and that frightened me a bit. "But they wouldn't listen," he went on. " 'Stay at home,' they said. 'You did your bit the last time. You got the medals to prove it.' " He looked away from me then, shaking his head. "Medals. They don't mean nothing. If only they knew. If only they knew."

I thought that was all he was going to say, but it wasn't. "Well, anyway, I did what they said. Got no choice, had I? But what can you do, with all them bombs coming down, houses blowed to bits, schools, hospitals, and those people killed, hundreds of 'em. Kids your age, babies. We were pulling out dozens of them, and most of them already dead. What's the use of that? You got to fight them. We should have had guns firing at them, knocking them out of the sky. We should have had planes up there shooting them down. Hundreds of bombers they sent over, set the whole city on fire, and all I could do was run around the streets blowing whistles and pulling people out . . ." He stopped then, too upset to go on.

I didn't know what to say, so I said nothing and looked out of the window. The train rattled on through the countryside, the telegraph poles whipping by. I counted a hundred of them before I got bored with it. Raindrops were chasing each other down the windows. I was looking up at the clouds then, watching the smoke from the train rising up, becoming part of them—now part of a roaring lion cloud, then a map of Britain cloud, then more like a one-eyed giant's face. It was a deep dark eye, a moving eye. It took me some moments to realize that the giant's eye was an airplane. By the time I knew and understood that properly, I found I couldn't make out the giant's face in the cloud anymore. It was just a cloud with an airplane flying out of it.

That was the moment I felt something stinging my eye. I knew at once it was grit from the open window. I could feel the sharpness of it. No amount of rubbing or blinking could seem to get it out, however hard I tried. It was stuck fast, somewhere deep in the corner of my eye. My finger couldn't get it out, blinking couldn't, nothing could. Everything I did was only making it worse, making it hurt more.

The stranger leaned forward then, took my hand, and pulled it gently away. "That won't help, son," he said. "Let me have a go. I'll get it out for you. Hold steady now, there's a good lad. Head back." He was grasping my shoulder, holding me firmly. Then he was trying to prise my eyelid open with his thumb. It was hard not to pull away, not to wince, not to blink. I could feel the corner of his handkerchief against my eyeball. I was blinking now. I couldn't help myself. It took a while, but suddenly it was over. He was sitting back, smiling at me, showing me triumphantly the black speck of grit on his handkerchief.

"See? What goes in always comes out," he said. "You'll be fine now." And I could tell from my blinking he was right. It was gone. I kept checking afterward, blinking again and again to be quite sure.

That's what I was still doing a little while later, as I was looking out of the window, which was how I saw the plane coming down out of the clouds. But it was much lower now than it had been before, and closer too. A fighter! And it was coming right toward us!

"Spitfire!" I cried, stabbing at the window with my finger. "Look! Look!" Ma was awake at once, all three of us now at the window.

"That ain't no Spitfire, son," said the stranger. "That's a flaming Messerschmitt 109, that is. German fighter. And it's diving, attacking. Away from the window! Now!"

3

H E GRABBED US BOTH AND PULLED US DOWN onto the floor of the carriage. There came a sudden roaring overhead, the sound of guns blazing, of shattering glass, of screaming, of the train whistling, gathering furious speed all the time. I was up on my knees, wanting to look out again, to see what was happening, but the stranger pulled me down again and held me there. "He'll be back," he said. "Stay put where you are, you hear me!" He was covering Ma and me now, his arms around us both, holding us to him, hands over our heads, protecting us.

He was right about the plane. Only moments later it was back and attacking again. We heard a bomb exploding and the repeated *rattattattatt rattattatt* of firing, and with it came the whining and the roaring of the plane's engine as it passed overhead. And all the while, the train raced on, faster, faster, until we were plunged into the sudden blackness of a tunnel. The brakes went on, hard, so shrill and loud that it hurt my ears. We found ourselves thrown violently together, squeezed half up against the seat and half underneath it. The squealing of the brakes seemed to go on forever, and all the while the stranger clung on to us tightly, until at long last the train came to a shuddering, hissing halt, and we were lying together there in the darkness. It felt almost as if the train and ourselves were breathing in unison, panting, all of us trying to calm down. The carriage was thick with darkness, pitch-black.

"Don't like tunnels," I said, trying my best not to sound as frightened as I was. "How long we going to be in here, Ma?"

"Best place for us just at the moment, son," the stranger told me. "And we're safe enough, that's for sure. We got a lot to thank the train driver for. He'll stay in here long as it takes, I reckon. Don't you worry, son." He was helping me to my feet and sitting me down. I felt Ma's arm come around me. She knew what I was going through. It wasn't the German plane or the shooting that terrified me—that had been exciting. It was the dark, this thick solid wall of blackness all around me, closing in on me, enveloping me. Ma knew I couldn't stand it, that I had to have the light on outside my bedroom door at night, as well as the lamp in the street outside. I felt a sob of fear rising in my throat and swallowed it, but it came back up again and again, like hiccups of terror that would not stop.

"It's the dark," Ma explained. "Barney don't like it, never has."

"Nor me neither," said the stranger. And as he spoke there was a sudden flicker of light in the darkness, then an orange flame, which lit up his face and his smile, then the whole carriage. "Smoke a pipe, don't I?" he went on. "So I always have my box of matches handy. Swan Vestas— you know, the ones with the swan on the box." He showed me. It rattled when he shook it. "See? Good they are, last longer." At once the panic in me subsided, and I knew it would not start again, just so long as the match lasted.

"The thing is, son," the stranger went on, "I reckon we're going to have to be in here for quite a while. If I was the engine driver, I'd sit tight in this tunnel till I was certain that plane—and I think maybe there was two of them, or more, who knows?—until I was quite sure they'd gone. They saw us go in here, right? So they could be waiting around up there for us to come out. Like I told you, what goes in comes out, and they know it." His face leaned in closer to me. "Trouble is, Barney, a match don't last forever, even a Swan Vestas match, and they last a lot longer than most. So I got to save them up a bit. I've got . . . one, two, three, four left—after this one, and this one's going out already, isn't it? So sooner or later, I got to blow it out, else I'll burn my fingers. But all you got to do is to ask me to light up another one, and it's done. Easy as pie. Only you won't need it, will you, son? Because you know your Ma's there and I'm here. So you're not alone. That's the thing about darkness, son. Makes you feel all alone. But you're not, are you?"

"I suppose," I said. He was looking right into my eyes. It felt as if he was breathing courage into me, through his eyes, through his smile. Then he blew out the match. We were suddenly in the dark again. I didn't like it, but somehow it didn't matter, not as much as I thought it would, as it had before.

"He's a brave boy, my Barney," said Ma. "Isn't he?"

"He certainly is, missus," the stranger replied. "And that's a fact. Reckon we'd better close the window," he said. I could hear him getting up, pulling up the window. "We don't want the carriage full of smoke, do we? The tunnel will be full of it soon enough."

"Trouble is, it'll get all hot and stuffy in here," said Ma. "But you're right, stuffy's a lot better than smoky."

We must have sat there for quite some time in the darkness, none of us speaking, before the stranger spoke up. "We got to pass the time somehow," he began. "You know what we used to do in the trenches, in the last war? Most of the time in a war, you know what you do? You sit around waiting for something to happen, hoping it won't. It's the waiting that was always the worst of it. We'd be hunkered down in our dugout, scared silly, waiting for the next Whizzbang to come over—beastly things they were. Or we'd be waiting for 'stand-to' in the early mornings. We had to be ready on 'stand-to,' see, cos that's when Fritz liked to attack. First light, out of the sun, out of the mist. And you know what we'd do sometimes? We'd tell each other stories—in the dark of the dugout it was often—just like it is now. We could do that now if you like. What d'you think, son?"

"Only if they're exciting, like Grandpa's, eh, Barney?" Ma replied, answering for me as usual. She was right though. I did like stories, but only when things happened fast and furious, shipwrecks and pirates and treasure, and wizards and hobgoblins, and wolves and tigers, stories of desert islands and jungles and football. Grandpa knew what I liked, and he told his stories so well that I believed every word, and I always hated them to be over. Somehow, some way, he always managed to weave into his stories a horse, called Big Black Jack, or a football match with Coventry City winning, and I loved that. Made it real for me, somehow.

"Well," the stranger said, "your grandpa isn't here, and I'm sure I couldn't tell stories as good as his anyway. But I could try, couldn't I? Give it a go. No pirates though, no desert islands or hobgoblins, and all that, I'm afraid. Not much good at making things up. But I could tell you a true story if you like, and what's more, a true story no one's heard before. How would that be? You like true stories, son?"

"Course he does," said Ma, with a laugh. I could feel something embarrassing was coming before it did. "My Barney, he likes all sorts of stories. Even been known to tell his own, from time to time." She nudged me meaningfully then. "And he's good at it too. Not true ones, of course. Tells us his little fibs, his little porky pies sometimes, don't you, Barney? We all do that, I suppose. We shouldn't, of course, but we do. Anyway, we'd love to hear your story, wouldn't we, Barney? And like you say, it'll pass the time while we're stuck in here. Bit hot and stuffy already, isn't it?"

"All right then," the stranger began, after a while. "Here's my story. Well, not exactly *my* story. About a pal of mine, a best friend you could call him, I suppose. I knew him better than anyone else in the whole world."

"What was his name?" I asked.

There was a pause.

"William Byron," he said. "But that wasn't his proper name. He didn't know his proper name. That was the name they gave him. He was just Billy to his friends, Billy Byron to everyone else."

PART TWO

———— ✦ ————

BILLY BYRON

4

"I SUPPOSE YOU COULD SAY I'VE KNOWED THIS Billy Byron just about all of my life," the stranger began. "We growed up together, Billy and me, same street, same town, same orphanage, same school, St. Jude's Elementary School. Down the end of Mulberry Road."

"Barney goes to St. Jude's," Ma exclaimed. "Don't you, Barney? Or he did, anyways."

"Well I never," he said. "Small world. Strange, eh? St. Jude's. Mulberry Road. Almost like we was meant to meet. S'where our orphanage was too, Mulberry Road. Mulberry Road Kids, they called us."

"I remember that orphanage from way back," Ma

went on. "They knocked it down years ago. Built houses there, and a shop, Mrs. McIntyre's place. And now that's gone too."

There was torchlight dancing suddenly along the corridor outside. The door slid open. "Guard here, madam. Just making sure you're all right," came a voice. The torch flashed round the carriage, then it was lighting up his face and his peaked cap for a moment as he spoke. "Won't be long stuck in here, don't suppose."

"Anyone hurt?" Ma asked. "In the other carriages?"

"Don't think so," said the guard. "Not so far as I know anyway."

"How long are we going to be here?" Ma said. "We got to change trains in London. We can't be late, you know. We're going down to Cornwall."

"Lucky you," replied the guard. "An hour maybe, at most, madam. Sorry about this, but our Mr. Hitler will have his little games, won't he? Be back later. Sit tight."

And he was gone, closing the door behind him and leaving us plunged into darkness again.

"Where was I now?" said the stranger. "Hardly started my story, had I?"

"You was in the orphanage down Mulberry Road," Ma told him.

"That's right, so I was. My dad put me in there when Ma died. Then he went off. Never saw him again. Good riddance, I say. Still, the orphanage weren't a bad sort of a place. Gave us our names, roof over our heads, food in our bellies. But not much else. Cold at nights, and the food were terrible. But school was all right. They teased us orphanage kids something rotten, of course. Mulberry Road Snotties, they called us. But Billy and me, we didn't mind. Sticks and stones and all that. We done everything together, bunked off together, got stood in the corner together, got whacked together. Happy-go-lucky, you'd call him; a cheerful sort of a Charlie.

"Always liked to draw, did Billy, even then. Birds; he liked birds best. Blackbirds, robins, crows. He could do them all—and people too. One time or another, he must've drawn just about everyone in that school, teachers as well, and sometimes they didn't like that. They thought he was cheeking them, but he wasn't. He was just drawing them. We left school the same day, walked out of the orphanage the same day too, worked together in a hotel looking after the boiler, and the garden, painting and decorating—odd jobs. Lived in the place too, in a little room up in the attic. Weren't treated like orphans no more, like slaves instead. They let us have one holiday in two years. One day, that's all. Went to Bridlington."

"We've been there!" I said. "I got a cockleshell from there, from the beach." I thought of our house then, all bombed out, and my special cockleshell, and my bus, and my tin soldiers. I wouldn't see any of them again.

"Lot in common, you and me," the stranger went on. "Bridlington—lovely place, eh? Best fish and chips I ever had. Sat there on the beach, looking out to sea and longed to go there, to see the world beyond, over the horizon. Billy picked up a piece of jet there, off the beach, shining black it was, called it his lucky pebble. Was lucky too, most of the time. But I'm getting ahead of meself here.

"Anyway, it was after that one day off we got thinking. We was right fed up with slaving away in that hotel. Had enough of it, quite enough. Then I met this soldier in the park, by the bandstand, one Sunday—well, we both did, Billy and me. This soldier, he was playing in the band. And we got talking to him, and he said how he'd been all over the world in the army, Africa, Egypt, China once. And where had Billy and me been? Bridlington. Billy'd got no family, nor me neither. We didn't much like stoking boilers and digging gardens and painting doors and not having hardly a penny to show for it. And that soldier told us you got all the food you could eat in the army, good nosh, and for free too. So the long and short of it is, we signed up for the army. They gave us uniforms and rifles, taught us how to go marching up and down, shoot a bit, how to polish boots and badges and keep our kit just so, and then we'd go marching up and down again. But that soldier in the park had been right; the food was good and regular and free. And soldiering was a whole lot better than working all day, it was, except there was always someone bellowing at us, telling us what to do, and mostly what not to do. Something like the orphanage really, when I come to think about it. But we had lots of pals, and we were all in it together. All a bit of a lark, it was.

"Then one day, we were all packed into trains, with our rifles and in full kit. And a few hours later we found ourselves marching through the streets, the band playing, and everyone cheering us and waving flags. Felt like we was proper heroes, we did. And then up the gangplank we went onto this great ship. All one big adventure, that's what we thought it was going to be. Only just as soon as the ship put to sea we were all sick as dogs, Billy too. But he kept smiling through—that's how he was. A cheery old card, always the jolliest of us all, always chipper, and always drawing too. Could hardly write a word, Billy. But my, how he loved to draw!

"I tell you, I'd never seen the sea before. But when I did, I never wanted to see it after! Do you know what? It never stops moving under your feet, and that churns your stomach something horrible. So it were quite a relief, I can tell you, when after weeks of that heaving sea we found ourselves on dry land again, and marching again, even if they were still shouting at us all the time. We were in Africa. South Africa.

"Long way from where your dad is, son. But Africa all the same. We was traveling the world. The sun was shining, and everything seemed to be just tickety-boo, 'ceptin the flies and the bellyache."

"Tickety-boo?" I asked him, puzzled. "What's that?"

"S'when you feel fine," he told us, "when there's nowt

to worry about. We were all happy as skylarks, happy as Larrys—tickety-boo. So we did get to go to Africa, just like that soldier on the bandstand had promised we would. We saw giraffes and lions and elephants and all sorts. You should see the sun out there when it's setting, huge and red, and so close you could almost reach up and touch it. Didn't do no fighting though. So instead they had us doing more marching up and down, more larking about, more sitting about. Happy days they was, when I think about them now. All the food we needed, lots of pals, and sunshine that warmed you right through. Billy drew whatever he could, animals now mostly, insects and trees and flowers, and the birds of course. Vultures, eagles. He was never happier than when he was sitting outside our tent and drawing. You should see Billy's sketchbooks—there's just about all of Africa in some of those books.

"Then before we knew it—it was 1914 by this time— we found ourselves back on a ship again, steaming out of Cape Town and homeward across that same heaving hor- rible sea. We were going home because the war in Europe had started, against the Germans. The kaiser had a huge great army and so he'd gone marching into Belgium. So to save brave little Belgium we had to fight him. We needed all the soldiers we could get, and that included us. We weren't worried, excited more like. No more sitting about for no good reason. No more marching up and down for no good reason. Billy was keen as mustard, he was, looking forward to it. Well, we all were. We were soldiers, weren't we? We'd soon sort Fritz out. We did lots of larking about, lots of singing on that ship—when we weren't feeling seasick, that is. We none of us knew what we were going to, and thinking back, I s'pose that was just as well."

5

"BILLY WAS UP ON DECK MOST OF THE TIME—you don't get so seasick up there, he said—drawing whales and dolphins and suchlike. But he loved albatrosses best, because they floated on the air, hovering, their wings hardly moving. They stayed still up there for him; made them easier to draw.

"Anyway, soon enough he had to put his sketchbook away, because once we landed we were marching up through Belgium. The war wasn't going well—we'd been told that much. But we hadn't seen it. We were still a bunch of happy-go-lucky lads, still larking about, still singing, Billy most of all. Quite a soldier he was, smart, never lagging behind, never out of step, first to volunteer for even the worst jobs.

"The sound of the guns was getting closer all the time. Convoys of ambulances passed us by and we could see they were full of wounded men. And there were carts too, piled high with furniture and belongings, a cow or a horse tied on behind sometimes, and whole families shuffling along the road, exhausted, babies and children crying. That were a pitiful sight, I can tell you. That soon stopped all the singing and the larking about. We marched on through deserted villages that lay in ruins, horses and mules lying dead and swollen by the side of the road. And once, in a roofless church, we saw hundreds of stretchers and empty coffins piled up against the wall. We all knew by now who those stretchers and coffins were likely to be for.

"Later on, when we got to camp, Billy got out his sketchbook and drew those coffins. It wasn't loping giraffes and soaring vultures, not the big round sun over Africa, nor whales in the ocean, nor albatrosses he was drawing now— it was the face of a wounded soldier in the back of an ambulance, it was a bent old woman leading a horse or cow along the road. And then one evening, he drew the little girl, the girl that was to change Billy's life forever, and he never even knew who she was, nor where she came from.

"We were all tramping through a village—a place called Poperinghe it was, just outside Ypres in Belgium—when he saw her by the side of the road, a little girl. She was sitting there hugging her knees, rocking herself, and whimpering. We all saw her as we came marching by. She was barefoot, shivering, and you could see there was no hope left in her. She wasn't the first we had seen like that. But she looked so alone in the world. Billy was marching along, like we all were. But he suddenly broke ranks and ran back to her. The sergeant bellowed at him. Billy took no notice of him. The column slowed and came to a halt, despite all the sergeant's shouting and cursing at us to pick up the step and move on. Everyone stood there and looked on as Billy crouched down beside the girl, talking to her, trying to comfort her. There was no comforting her, though.

"Billy didn't think twice about it, he just picked the girl up and carried her.

"Now the major was riding back along the column on his horse, yelling at Billy to put the girl down and get back

in line. Billy stood there, calm as you like, while the officer yelled at him, giving him a piece of his mind from high
up on his horse.

" 'What d'you think we're here for, Private?' he ranted
on. 'Do you think we're here to nursemaid these people?
If you want to save that girl, if you want to save them all,
you save your strength for the Germans. You drive them
back to Germany. That's the way to save her and thousands of others like her. Now put her down, Private, and
join the ranks.'

" 'Fraid I can't do that, sir,' Billy replied quietly. 'I'll
fight the Germans like you say, but first we got to get this
girl to a field hospital. She'll die else. She needs help, a doctor, sir, and we got doctors, haven't we? She's as weak as a
kitten, sir. I can't leave her. She's got no ma, no pa, she's all
alone. This war done that to her. Everyone should have
a ma and a pa and a home. She got nothing. That ain't
right, sir. And we got to do something about it. Can't just
leave her there, can we, sir?'

"That silenced the major. He didn't argue, nor did
the sergeant. So Billy joined the column again and carried
that little girl to the nearest field hospital, wrapped up in

his greatcoat, and talking to her all the while as he marched. Then everyone stopped to rest while Billy laid her down on a stretcher and held her hand for a few moments. Stretcher bearers came and took her away, into the hospital tent.

"None of us could forget that little girl afterward, least of all Billy. That girl was what made him do what he did later—he always told us that. It was partly what the major had shouted at him from high on his horse that day, but mostly it was because of the look in the girl's eyes as he said good-bye to her at the field hospital. They were eyes full of pain and hopelessness. If he understood her right— and he couldn't ever be sure of it afterward—he thought she was trying to tell him that her name was Christine. That was all he knew about her. He drew her again and again in the weeks and months that followed, wrote her name at the bottom of every picture. The more he drew her, the more he thought about her, talked about her, the more sure he was what he should do about her and about all children like her, alone and orphaned by this war.

"He was going to do all in his power to finish this war as soon as possible, to end the hurt, to stop the pain.

"Almost at once we found ourselves in the front line, down in the trenches for the first time. The least said about the trenches, the better. Moles is supposed to live in the ground, worms maybe, but not men. To be honest, not much happened, not at first. The odd shell came over, and there was always snipers, so you had to keep your head down. We was frightened, course we were. We knew Fritz was out there, and out to get us, just a hundred yards away down in their trenches on the other side of no-man's-land. You could hear them talking and laughing, hear their music playing sometimes. But we didn't see them, and we knew better than to stick our heads up and have a look. That's what their snipers were waiting for. First man I ever saw killed died that way. Harold Merton, he was called, I remember. Only eighteen, he was. Quiet sort of lad, unless he was singing. He loved to sing. Sang in the church choir at home. Manchester lad, he was; supported United. He had a great voice too. One moment I was talking to him, the next he was dead.

"So we sat in our dugout and smoked our Woodbines, wrote letters, played cards, told our stories—much like I'm doing now. Billy drew his pictures, of us sometimes, good they were too—and we ate stew and more stew and more stew, and bread and marmalade if you were lucky, Tickler's marmalade. And we slept, or tried to. Fritz seemed to know just when we were dropping off to sleep and would send a Whizzbang over to wake us up. We had to take our turns at sentry duty, of course, and at dawn every morning we were all on the firestep on 'stand-to.' That's when Fritz liked to attack, at dawn, out of the half-dark, out of the mist, out of the rising sun. So we had to be ready for him, bayonets fixed, one round up the spout. And Billy was always out of the dugout first and up on the firestep, ready. It was almost as if he was hoping Fritz would come, as if he couldn't wait to have a go at them.

"Some nights, when it was dark enough, we'd be sent out on a patrol, with an officer or sergeant or a corporal in charge. You had to climb out, crawl across no-man's-land on your belly, not making a sound, then wriggle through their wire and drop down into their trenches. You had to bring back one of them for questioning, that's what we was ordered to do. They'd give you a double ration of rum if you volunteered, but even so no one wanted to go, except Billy, and Billy didn't even like rum. He only liked beer.

He volunteered every time, never seemed to bother him. 'Bonkers Billy,' some called him, but he didn't mind. He wasn't bonkers, of course, we all knew that, not mad at all, and not brave either. It was like he said. He just wanted to get the war over with as quick as he could, so that no more children would be orphaned, like little Christine in his sketchbook.

"That first time when the whistle blew, and we went out over the top, all of us together, into the crackle and rattle and spit of machine-gun fire and rifle fire, into the shelling and the smoke and the screaming of battle, Billy led the way and we all followed. We was scared stiff—and Billy was too. He joked about it, said he had his lucky black pebble from Bridlington in his pocket, that he'd be all right. But I reckon he'd worked out what we'd all worked out, that it didn't much matter whether you were first or last out of the trenches, whether you walked or you ran; that once you were up there and out in no-man's-land, it was just luck. You can't dodge bullets and shrapnel. They either hit you or they don't. You either die quick like Harold Merton had, or you don't. You could get through without a scratch. You could get yourself a little wound, get patched up in the field hospital, have a few days recovering, and then be sent back up into the line; or you could get 'a blighty one,' when it were a more serious wound, and get sent home to hospital.

"'Lap of the Gods,' Billy always said it was, and you couldn't win this war and get it over with by worrying yourself about it. You just got to get on with it. You see friends die, like poor Harold, and it could give you nightmares, give you the shakes. But every time Billy saw someone wounded, every time he lost a pal, it just made him all the more determined to keep going, to kill or capture as many Fritzis as he could. For him, that was the only way to end the war.

"As it turned out, Billy got himself a blighty wound on the Somme in October 1916. Shrapnel in the leg. At the field hospital he told the doctor he wanted them to patch him up there and then so he could get back into the fight. When they said he couldn't, he tried walking out of the hospital, but they brought him back. The doctor said he was going home, that it were a bad wound, deep and dangerous, that he needed a proper hospital back home. And that was that. So for a while, Billy lay there in hospital back in England, in a big house in the country—in Sussex, it was—with deer in the park outside his window, swans on the lake. All the time, he was willing his leg to heal. He drew the deer, the swans—drew Christine again, drew his pals—to remind him why he had to get back to the trenches.

"When he slept it was little Christine's face that haunted his dreams. He wanted to get back to the war and back to his pals too. His pals were his family now, all the family he'd ever had, and he wanted to be with them."

6

"BUT BY THE TIME BILLY CAME BACK TO THE fighting a month or so later, a lot of his pals weren't there. They'd had a rough time of it while he'd been away. Lots of them dead, or missing, or wounded. Faces not there anymore, nearly half of Billy's new family gone, just like that. And Billy blamed himself. He should've been there to look out for them, instead of lying in bed in that hospital, in that grand house back home. He belonged here, with them. More and more now, it wasn't just for that little Christine he was doing his fighting—it was for his pals too, those who were left. He wouldn't ever leave them again, no matter what.

"So, when in the winter of 1917, near Passchendaele, it was, Billy was wounded again—a bullet in the arm this time—and they tried to send him home again to England, to a proper hospital, he just walked out of the field hospital at nighttime when no one was about and made his way back to his pals. When the doctors discovered he was missing, they thought he must have deserted, and the military police went after him to arrest him. They found him in the end in the place they least expected to find him—back in the trenches with his pals. You can't hardly arrest someone for deserting if he deserts back to the front line, can you? So they left him be where he was.

"Over the months Billy seemed to care less and less whether he lived or died. If there was someone lying wounded out there in no-man's-land, he'd fetch him in. If everything looked hopeless, like Fritz was going to break through the line and surround them, Billy went on fighting, and so did his pals. He wasn't going to let Fritz win, even when things looked bad, when it looked for a while as if they would. We were somewhere near Cambrai the next spring, close to a canal, as I remember it. The tide of the war had turned. We were winning. We were going forward. We had the Fritz on the run, or so we thought. But Fritz don't run easy. Say what you like about them, one thing I learned in that war was that they were every bit as brave as we were. They may have been retreating, but they stopped and fought wherever they could.

"Anyway, one morning, we found ourselves stuck good and proper. They had us pinned down. Machine gun, it was. We couldn't go forward and we couldn't go back. So Billy says he needs two men to go with him, and the others should stay where they are and give us covering fire. So they go forward, the three of them 'to sort Fritz out,' he says. And that's what he does. Bonkers Billy goes charging forward with the other two, and somehow none of them get hit. Pretty soon they're chucking bombs, grenades, down into the German trenches and the machine gun stops firing. And lo and behold, Fritz throws in the towel. They're putting up their hands and surrendering, twenty, maybe thirty of them, throwing down their rifles, just like that. Dozens of prisoners we took that day, and not a scratch on any one of us. Ruddy miracle it was, begging your pardon, missus."

Ma didn't reply, and I knew from the rhythm of her

breathing beside me that she must be fast asleep. I was feeling sleepy too, but I'd been forcing myself to stay awake. I
really wanted to hear what was going to happen to Billy in
the stranger's story. The carriage was as black as the tunnel
outside the window, but it didn't bother me, not anymore.

"I think Ma's asleep," I told him.

"Shall I light another match, Barney?" he asked me.
"Or you all right now?"

"Think so," I told him. In fact I had by now completely
forgotten about the dark.

"You want me to finish my story, son? Don't want to
wake her up, do I?"

"Didn't Billy get a medal for doing all that?" I asked.

"He did indeed, son," he went on. "And not just one.
He kept on getting medals too. Like his pals said, Billy only
had to sneeze and they'd give him a medal. They joked
about it, teased him fit to bust sometimes. But he didn't
mind, because he knew that deep down they were proud
of him, because he was one of them, and he didn't pretend
any different, no matter how famous he became. And he
did become famous too. Had his picture in the paper more
than once. The newspapers made a bit of a fuss of Billy

every time they gave him a medal. But he didn't take no notice of all that, and neither did his pals.

"The army wanted to promote him, give him a stripe, make him a lance corporal. But he didn't want that. He told them, thank you very much, but he was quite happy as he was, being a private, like his pals. But they kept on giving him medals, whether he liked it or not. Sometimes it was for going out and rescuing one of his pals under fire. And then once when there weren't enough stretcher bearers to carry back the worst of the wounded, he carried one of his pals on his back, three miles or more it was, all the way back to the field hospital, the shells landing all around him. He got another medal for that too.

"But Billy didn't do it for the medals. He just wanted it to end, get out of uniform, to stoke his boiler in that hotel, sleep in his cold little attic room again and draw his pictures. That hotel he had hated so much seemed like a paradise to him now. He wanted to forget all about the fighting and the trenches, all about little Christine by the side of the road and the sadness in her eyes. He wanted not to have to think anymore of his pals lying there stretched out on the ground looking up into the sky with empty eyes, unseeing eyes. He didn't care about living or dying by now. He was tired, so tired. We all were. We just wanted it to be over, for there to be peace. The quicker the better for all the little Christines, for all the soldiers, for all of us.

"Which was why Billy done what he done that day at the end of September 1918—just a couple of weeks before the end of the war, though of course he didn't know that at the time. No one knew when exactly it would end, but everyone knew by now that peace couldn't be far off. Every day now the army was on the move, getting up out of the trenches where we had been stuck for so long, advancing everywhere, and everywhere Fritz was falling back.

"It happened near a village called Marcoing—never sure how you say that name—'Marcong' we called it. That's the trouble with foreign names—French, Belgians, they don't pronounce their words like we do, which is fair enough, I s'pose, when you come to think about it. Anyway, Billy and all of us were trying to capture this little village. We didn't know it, but Fritz was well dug in, in their trenches, in amongst the buildings too, what was left of them. And they were letting us have it, firing at us with everything they'd got—machine guns, rifles. Some of the lads were hit at once; the rest of us took cover. Not Billy, of course. He crawled forward, got as close as he could and threw his bombs, which knocked out the machine gun. He was wounded, but that didn't stop him. Then, fired up by his example, the whole company was up and at them. There was a lot of killing that day, and it wasn't pretty. It never is. Don't let no one ever tell you different, son.

"But the battle wasn't over yet. We had to get across the canal to attack Fritz on the other side. They were firing at Billy all the time from across the canal, but he didn't pay no attention to that. He just got on with what he had to do. He was laying planks across the canal, to make a sort of bridge, so we could get over. We were firing and firing, keeping their heads down as best we could. And that's how we got across that canal, on Billy's planks. But Fritz wasn't finished yet. They came at us from all sides, trying to drive us back into the canal.

"Billy wasn't having none of it. He weren't going to retreat. So Billy and all of us, we stuck it out. Billy was wounded twice more, but nothing was going to stop him now. He was going to finish the war here and now, by himself if necessary, get it done, for good and all. It was kill or be killed, that's all there was to it. And they were the enemy. After a war's over, you can talk about the rights and wrongs of it, but in the middle of a battle, soldiers don't ask themselves those questions.

"But once a battle's over, well, that's a different matter. And by now the fight was over. There were dead and wounded all around us, our lads some of them, but mostly theirs. That's when you look at what you done. We had won, but it didn't feel like winning, never does. No joy in it. No triumph. All we felt was relief. We were alive—for the time being anyway. We had got away with it.

"We had taken prisoners, lots of them, over thirty, if I remember right. Exhausted they were, hungry, looked more like ghosts. 'Spect we all did. The officer surrendered to Billy, saluted and handed him his pistol. Like all of us, he knew it was Billy who had won this battle almost single-handed. We checked them all over to make sure they had no hidden weapons, no grenades, knives. We had nothing to say to them, and they had nothing to say to us. We gave them cigarettes. They didn't seem such a bad lot. Young, some of them, just boys they looked like. You felt a bit sorry for them. It was quiet all around, so quiet, like a calm after a storm.

"Then we see this Fritz soldier coming out of the smoke, no more than twenty yards away he was, and he's holding a rifle, not pointing it at us, holding it. Then he just turns and walks off. Billy shouts at him to stop and he does. There's half a dozen rifles pointing at him, but Billy tells us not to shoot. Pointing his pistol at him, he orders the Fritz soldier to drop his rifle, showing him what to do. But the soldier just stands there holding it, like he's in a daze. A little fellow, bareheaded he was, no cap, his uniform covered in mud. He stands there, looking back at us, staring, like he's looking through us. You can see in his face he's just waiting for the bullet. He pushes his dark hair back off his forehead with the flat of his hand, stands straight, rifle at his side. But he won't put it down, and we're all ready to shoot him. That's when Billy says it.

" 'No,' he tells us. 'Don't shoot him, lads. There's been enough killing done today. They're beaten. He's going home, let him go home. He's not going to shoot us, not now. War's over, and he knows it.' And then Billy walked toward him, calling out to him: 'Go home, Fritz, it's over. The war is over. Go, before I change my mind.' "

"Then he lifts his pistol high and fires it into the air,

deliberately over the soldier's head. The Fritz soldier just nods, looks at him for a moment or two, lays his rifle down, turns and walks off, and we watch him go, glad we haven't killed him, because we all knew as we stood there that Billy was right, that there was no point in killing another one. To all of us, that soldier walking away, going home, meant only one thing—that the war was over and done with, and that soon we'd be going home ourselves.

"Billy bent down and picked up the spent cartridge from the ground. 'That's the last shot I'm ever going to fire in this war,' he said. 'And it wasn't in anger, and it didn't kill anyone. I'm going to keep it always, to remind me.'

"For what he did that day at Marcoing they gave Billy the Victoria Cross—and they don't hand those out very often. Most of the people who get one are dead already, killed in action. By rights, Billy should have been too. But, as he always said, he had his lucky black pebble from the beach at Bridlington, so Lady Luck was on his side. After a month or so in hospital he was right as rain again—well, sort of as good as. He always walked with a bit of a limp after that. Anyway he was all fit and spruced up in his uniform at Buckingham Palace a few weeks later to receive his

Victoria Cross, which was pinned on his chest by King George V himself.

"The king said he was a great hero, that the country was proud of him. But he told the king that he was wrong. 'To be a hero,' he said, 'you got to be brave, sir, and I weren't any braver than anyone else.'

"He wanted to tell him that he didn't do it for king and country, that he did what he did for little Christine and for his pals. Just get the war over with, that's all he had in mind. But he weren't brave enough to tell the king that. Afterward he always wished he had been."

The stranger fell silent. I could feel Ma was still fast asleep, hear her breathing beside me. But now, with the story over—or that's what I thought—I found the blackness suddenly closing in on me. I wanted the story to go on, to take my mind off the darkness around me. "Is that all?" I asked him.

A sudden flame flared, lighting the carriage, lighting his face from under his chin. He was half smiling.

"I wish it was, son," he said. "There's more, I'm afraid. Lots more. But only three more matches."

PART THREE

———✦———

IF EVER A LOOK COULD KILL

7

"I THINK YOUR MA MUST BE SLEEPING." THE STRANGER spoke softly, leaning forward. "Don't want to wake her, do I?"

"I'm not asleep," said Ma, her eyes opening. "I've been listening to every word. Good story too, so far as it goes. But you haven't told us what happened to this Billy fellow, this friend of yours, after the war was over."

The match was burning down. He shook it out, plunging the carriage once more into darkness. "I was coming to that," he went on. "Just wanted to make sure you wasn't both fast asleep, that I wasn't talking to myself."

"How long we going to be in this tunnel, Ma?" I asked.

The darkness was really getting to me again now. Once that match had gone out, it was so dense, that darkness, so impenetrable. And I knew he only had three more matches left. "How long?" I said.

"Till it's safe to come out, I suppose," she said. "That plane can't hardly hurt us in here, can it, Barney? Safe as houses, we are." She patted my hand and squeezed it. "Isn't that right, mister?"

"Safer, I hope," the man replied. "Houses aren't very safe these days—not in Coventry anyway—if you know what I'm saying."

"You're right enough there," said Ma. "Barney's dad was in the last war too, y'know," she went on. "Not in the trenches like you was, like that Billy. He was in Palestine. He was there with horses. He knows horses. No one could handle Big Black Jack like he could. He's good with horses, isn't he, Barney? Growed up with them, worked with Grandpa delivering coal. Got a few medals too—not a Victoria Cross like your friend, mind. But we lost them too, in the bombing, like everything else. Only got what we stand up in, and a few bits and bobs in that suitcase above your head. Still, we're alive, and there's plenty that aren't in Coventry."

"That's true enough," the stranger said. "Don't think anyone knows how many were killed. Thousands, that's for sure."

"Don't bear thinking about," Ma went on. "Let's not talk about it, eh? Don't want to upset the boy, do we? So, what happened to this Billy then when he came home from the war? Where's he now? Has he joined up again this time like Barney's dad did? I didn't want him to, you know. Over forty he is. Too old to go, I told him, but he wouldn't listen." I could hear Ma's voice wavering, heard her opening her handbag and knew she was taking out her handkerchief. I think the stranger must have known it too because he went right on with his story.

"Billy wanted to join up, course he did," he began, "but they wouldn't let him, on account of his bad leg. Those old wounds of his never really healed. They said he was too old anyway, so they wouldn't pass him fit. He tried again and again, showed them his Victoria Cross, his Military Medal, his Distinguished Conduct Medal, all of them. But they wouldn't listen. They turned him down. And I can tell you, that upset Billy more than just about anything that ever happened to him before. And he had good reason to be upset, believe you me; and that's because he had more reason to want to join up than anyone else in this whole country, and that's because, as far as Billy was concerned, this whole war is his fault."

"What do y'mean?" Ma asked. "How could it be? It's lousy Adolf Hitler's fault, we all know that."

For some time, the stranger didn't reply. "That's true enough," he said. "And that's the trouble. I'd best tell you how it happened, I suppose, how come we're sitting here in this tunnel, how come there's a war on and what Billy has to do with it." He seemed to be thinking about what he was going to say for a very long time, before he began again.

"Well, after the last war was over, it turned out that Billy Byron was just about the most decorated private in the whole British Army; a great hero, who'd done this and done that. They made a huge fuss of him, but all he wanted was to be left alone. 'Bravest of the brave,' the newspapers called him, but he knew he wasn't, that the bravest of the brave had never come home, never worn any medals. They asked him to help carry the coffin of the Unknown Soldier into Westminster Abbey, with the king there and hundreds of thousands watching. On parade, with his medals on his chest—the whole army was proud of him, the regiment was proud of him, his pals were too. But Billy didn't feel proud. He couldn't help thinking about how it had been out there, the killing and the dying. There were reminders all around him. Every time he saw a soldier or a sailor sitting on a street corner begging, with no legs, or blind, or both; every time he saw a woman pass him in the street wearing black, it made him remember all he didn't want to remember.

"He stayed in the army for a while because they were his family, and he didn't want to leave them. But in the end Billy decided it was time to put the army behind him, and all the newspapers and the interviews—they wouldn't leave him alone. The army tried again and again to talk him into staying, but he'd had enough of it all. He handed in his uniform and left. He kept only a few mementos. He squirreled away some of his wartime bits and bobs, hid them in a large biscuit tin: photos of his pals, his medals, his lucky black pebble, the pistol the German officer had given him that day after the Battle of Marcoing and the spent cartridge. There were some things he didn't want to part with. He scarcely ever looked in that tin. He wanted to forget and get on with his life. But at the same time he wanted to remember. He had his sketchbooks too, and they were full of memories.

"He went back to the hotel, because jobs weren't easy to find, and any job was better than no job, even the hotel job. But he found it had closed down. Then he heard there were jobs in a car factory in Coventry, so he went there and got lucky. He tried to settle into work. But the trouble was that the war stayed in his head, the sights and sounds and smell of it, the sadness of it. It's the same for all of us who've fought in a war. You don't forget. You can't. You want to, but you can't. Billy would lie awake at nights, and he'd see that little girl's eyes in his mind. He'd find himself saying her name out loud sometimes. 'Christine, Christine.' He drew her often, and all the while he was wondering what might have happened to her, whether she'd survived the war and found somewhere to live, someone to look after her. He tried not to draw those memories of the war.

Instead he would walk the streets of Coventry, sketch the people, the children in the streets, the cats, the cathedral, the pigeons.

"He particularly loved to draw the pigeons. But then sometimes, even sitting outside the cathedral where there were always lots of pigeons about, he would find himself drawing a picture of a tank, or a gun, or a field hospital, for no good reason—and then he'd be drawing Christine, always little Christine. He couldn't seem to help himself.

"In the car factory, it had soon got about, of course, that Billy Byron was a bit of a hero from the war—someone had seen his picture in a newspaper. And for a while that set him apart from the others. Most of them had been to the war just like he had, and wanted to forget about it if they could. So once they'd got over the fact that one of their fellow workers had won the Victoria Cross, and once they realized Billy just wanted to get on with his work and have a quiet life, they didn't bother much about his medals anymore. And that was how Billy liked it. He just wanted to be left alone.

"The years passed, and all the time he was working, or back home in his room, Billy found himself thinking more and more about little Christine. Had she survived? What had happened to her? He had to find out, he had to know. He hadn't wanted ever to go back to the battlefields in France and Belgium. He never wanted to see them again. But he knew that the only place to start his search was where he had last seen her.

"So off he went, during his week's holiday in the summer of 1924 to Ypres, to Belgium, looking for that field hospital in Poperinghe where he had last seen Christine, all those years before."

8

"HE WALKED THE COBBLED STREETS, SAT IN THE cafés, looking for her everywhere he went. Of course she wasn't there, and nor was the field hospital. He couldn't really remember where it was. The town was being rebuilt. Nothing looked the same at all, except the square in the center, and the cafés there. Billy showed his drawings of Christine wherever he went. He wandered all the villages around, asking if anyone had known a little orphan girl called Christine. Wherever he went he passed the cemeteries, rows and rows of crosses, thousands upon thousands of them. He found Harold Merton's grave, and stood there over him in the rain, and tried to remember his face.

He couldn't. But he remembered the moment he died. There were trenches and craters wherever he looked, and many of the houses were still in ruins. But they were busy rebuilding everywhere, and in the fields the grass was growing where there had once been nothing but trenches and wire and mud. There were cows grazing, and sheep. That gave him heart. That gave him hope.

"But no one anywhere had heard of Christine, no one recognized her from his drawings. He was disappointed, but not surprised. They were drawings after all, not photographs, and anyway the drawings were of a little girl. Christine wouldn't be a little girl anymore.

"It was the last day and he was sitting in the town square in Ypres, outside a café drinking a glass of beer—he always remembered the beer from the war. A meal of egg and chips and beer was just about his only truly happy memory of his time as a soldier. He had his sketchbook out. He was drawing a cat that was sitting at his feet, gazing up at him, when he felt someone looking over his shoulder. It was the waitress. She spoke in broken English, asking if he was an artist.

" 'Not really,' he said, and as he spoke the pages of his sketchbook lifted in the wind and flipped over to a drawing he'd done that morning of Christine as he'd last seen her, lying on a stretcher, her name written underneath.

"The waitress was bending down, examining the drawings more closely. 'Who is this Christine?' she asked.

" 'Just a little girl I once knew,' he told her. 'It was a long time ago, in the war. She was an orphan, I think. I was a soldier then. I took her to a hospital.'

"She looked long and hard at the drawings, turning the pages and clearly becoming more and more interested all the time. Then she said quietly: 'You have done many pictures of her. I think perhaps I may know this girl. If I am right, I was at school with her after the war, in the convent. Yes, this is Christine, Christine Bonnet, I am sure of it. You draw her very well.'

" 'You know her!' Billy said. 'Where is she? Do you know where she lives?'

" 'Not where she lives. I do not know her well anymore, but I think she was a teacher in the same school we went to together. Maybe she still is. I don't know.'

"Billy was waiting outside the school gates that afternoon. He recognized Christine at once, as she came toward him wheeling her bicycle.

"'Hello, Christine,' he said. 'You won't remember me.' He did his best to explain, the words falling over themselves as they spilled out of him. She was taken aback at first. She didn't remember him, not exactly, but she could remember, she said, a soldier carrying her along the road, and the field hospital and the doctor there, and the convent afterward, where they had looked after her for the rest of the war. They walked and they talked. Billy had found his Christine.

"To cut a long story short, Billy came back to see her every summer for the next few years, and then she came to Coventry to see him. They were married, and were happy. Each had their sadnesses, of course, each had no family, but each was a comfort to the other. After a while Christine found a job teaching in the local school in Coventry, where very soon the children, she said proudly, were the only children in the whole country who could count to ten in her language, in Flemish. They wanted to have children of their own, but it didn't happen. Despite this, Billy and Christine were truly contented. They were alive, when so many they had known were not, and they had a home and a job to go to. And they had one another.

"But then the old war came back to haunt Billy, and in a manner he could never have expected or imagined."

The stranger paused then, taking a deep breath, almost as if he didn't want to go on.

"Is there going to be haunting then? Is it going to be a ghost story?" I asked him. "I like ghost stories."

"Shush, Barney," said Ma. "Don't interrupt the gentleman."

"No, son," he went on. "No ghosts in this story, I'm afraid. But in a way it was a haunting, a real live haunting, and it began in the cinema. Christine and Billy liked to go to the pictures. It was their great treat. They went as often as they could afford—adventure films were their favorites. Christine had taken quite a shine to a big Hollywood star called Douglas Fairbanks Jr."

"I like him too," said Ma. "Proper handsome he is."

"Just what Christine thought," the stranger went on. "Anything he was in she had to see. Anyway, they were walking past the cinema one Saturday afternoon, the Roxy it was, and there was his name up on the poster. 'Mr. *Robinson Crusoe*, starring Douglas Fairbanks Jr.' So they paid at the kiosk and went in to see it.

"The cinema was dark as the usherette showed them to their seats. Up on the screen, the newsreel was showing already. There was a sudden chorus of hooting and whistling and booing from all around them, and once Billy and Christine were sitting down, they soon discovered why. There he was, up on the screen, Adolf Hitler, the German *Führer*, and as usual he was working himself up into one of his rages. All of a lather he was, ranting and raving. Billy had heard him often enough on the wireless— everyone had—and he'd always switched him off, because he knew it upset Christine so much to have to listen to him. But now in the cinema, he couldn't switch him off. They both had to sit there and listen to him, whether they liked it or not.

"They didn't understand exactly what he was saying, of course, but like everyone else in the cinema, you got the gist of it, from the hysteria of his voice, from the hate in his eyes and those clenched fists of his punching the air. He was up there in his uniform on the podium at some huge torchlit rally, the kind everyone there had seen before, where there were thousands upon thousands of soldiers in the same coal-scuttle helmets Billy remembered so well from the war all those years before. The crowd was hanging on his every word, like they was all hypnotized or something. Then they were roaring their approval, mad with feverish adoration, they were. Like thunder their cheering was, every one of them arm-outstretched in that stiff, straight Nazi salute. And Hitler stood there basking in it all, wallowing in every moment of it, thumb hooked into his belt, saluting back, surveying his troops and looking for all the world like he was some Roman emperor.

"As Billy and Christine watched, both chilled to their hearts at what they were seeing, Hitler waved the crowds to silence, and on he went with his tirade, every sentence punctuated by wild gesticulations. But the people in the Roxy cinema that day weren't silenced. They were laughing at him, mimicking him, mocking him. And before long, Billy and Christine were laughing along with them, determined like everyone else there not to be cowed by this crazed maniac.

"Then—all of a sudden it was—there was no sound on the newsreel, just the pictures. Hitler was reduced to silence. There was only his face up there on the screen, contorted and full of fury, mouthing his hate. Every unheard word was somehow more fearful than ever before. The whole cinema fell silent. Looking up at him now, Billy didn't need to hear his voice to hear what he meant, to understand what he had in his mind. His face said it all. His eyes said it all, those dark staring eyes. They were looking at Billy now, right at him and only at him—that's what it felt like—and he could see the evil intent in them. If ever a look could kill.

"It was at that precise moment, as their eyes met in the cinema, that Billy felt he had met this man before, not on screen, but face to face. And when Hitler raised his hand and brushed his hair back from his forehead, he knew at once who it was, and where they had met, and remembered everything that had happened between them.

"Christine clutched his arm, looking away from the screen, then buried her head in Billy's shoulder. Billy realized that everyone in that cinema was feeling as she did. It was fear, the kind that gripped your body and soul and wouldn't leave you. No one whistled anymore, no one hooted, no one laughed. It was as if everyone in the cinema was holding their breath, waiting for what was to come, dreading the horror of it, but knowing that there was nothing that could stop it, because this man, this Hitler, was going to make it happen. But Billy knew more. All the while Billy looked up into his eyes and could not look away. All the while he was wondering if what had come into his mind could possibly be true. The more he looked into those eyes, the more he realized that it was, that there could be no doubt about it. That man, that warmonger, was up there now, able to spew out his hatred only because Billy had spared his life all those years before, after the Battle of Marcoing."

The stranger fell silent. The train breathed on, as if it had been listening with us. As if it was waiting to hear more. In the silence of the carriage, the darkness closed in again around me. I grasped Ma's hand and held it tight.

"Well I never!" said Ma. "Would you believe it?"

"If Billy believed it," the stranger told her, "then I do too."

"Could you light another match?" I asked him. "It keeps getting darker in here."

I heard the stranger fiddling with the matchbox, heard it slide open. I was longing all the while for the light.

"Here goes," he said. The match struck once, twice. Sparked. But no light. "Third time lucky," he muttered.

And it was too. The flame flared, lighting his face, lighting the darkness, driving it away.

9

"THERE, BARNEY DEAR," SAID MA. "IT'S ALL RIGHT, SEE? Nothing to worry about." But there soon was, because the light was dying all the time. And then it was gone altogether. "Go on with the story, mister," Ma said. "Barney'll like that, won't you? Make him feel better."

"Whatever you like, missus," he said, and began the story again.

"Billy had seen enough up on that screen," the stranger continued. "He just got up and walked out of the cinema. Christine went after him. Out in the street Billy walked on home not saying a word to her. Back home he sat in his chair all that evening and stared into the fire, still not speaking. He didn't touch his supper. Christine knew better than to ask him what the matter was. He would be like this from time to time. He'd often joke about his moods, afterward, when they were over—his 'glum time,' he called it. He liked to be left alone when he was like this. He would come out of it sooner or later and be himself again. Christine was used to it by now. It was the war that haunted him, she knew that much. She tried all she could to cheer him up, but nothing seemed to work.

"This time, she knew something was different. Billy's glum time went on day after day, week after week, for so long that Christine began to wonder if it would ever end. She wondered if he shouldn't go to see the doctor, but didn't like to suggest it. It would upset him, and he was upset enough already.

"It wasn't until one night a month or so later that he told her at last what had been making him like this. They were lying in bed, side by side, in the darkness—each of them knowing the other could not sleep—when Billy came out with it.

" 'It were him, Christine,' he said. 'In the Roxy, up on the screen that night. Can't be no mistake about it. I'd know those eyes anywhere. You can't forget them. He looked at me out of that newsreel just like he did all those years ago, in the war it was. And did you see how he pushed his hair away from his forehead, with the flat of his hand? He always does that, don't he? I never seen no one else do it like that. It were him. I know it was. It were that Hitler.'

"Christine didn't understand what he was talking about. In all the time they had been together, ten years or more by this time, he had scarcely ever spoken about the war. Neither of them had. She knew about his medals, of course, about how famous he'd been, years before—and she was proud of him too, prouder than he was—but she'd never seen them or asked to see them. The medals, like the memories, were hidden away, the war hardly ever mentioned these days. To talk of those terrible times was only to bring them back. They both longed for the memories to fade. They both wanted to look to the future, to forget the past. It had been, over the years, like an unspoken pact between them, never to speak of the war. But now, for the first time, Billy did.

"'I got something I have to tell you, to show you,' he said. He turned on the light, got out of bed, pulled the biscuit tin out from underneath it, where he kept his few bits and pieces from the war: the photographs of his pals, the pistol he had taken off a German officer who had surrendered to him at the Battle of Marcoing, his lucky black pebble from Bridlington he'd had in his pocket, that had kept him safe. There were his medals too, and the cartridge from the last bullet he had fired in the war, the warning shot he'd fired over that German soldier's head. An unknown German soldier then, but not anymore.

"He laid the medals out on the bed in front of her. 'This one is the Victoria Cross,' he explained to her. 'Don't look like much, do it? Not shining like the others. Plain old ribbon too. But this is the one all the fuss has been about. They gave me this one, the king did, because of a battle I was in, near the end of the war, it was, near a little village called Marcoing, not that there was much of it left. Well, the fighting was all over, and me and the lads had done what we had to do. There was lots of dead and wounded, ours and theirs, but more of theirs, and we had taken dozens of prisoners.

"'Anyhow, all of a sudden, we see this Fritz soldier and he's just standing there as the smoke clears, ten yards away, no more, rifle in his hand. And I tell the lads not to shoot, cos he don't look as if he's going to shoot us. And we're just looking at him and he's looking at us. It was so quiet, Christine. The quiet after a battle is the quietest quiet there is. None of us moved, not a muscle, nor did he; no one did. None of us spoke. Just stood there like we was all in a dream, like it wasn't real. And then I fire this pistol into the air and wave him away, tell him to go home. He nods at me, brushes his hair off his forehead, and walks off.

"'It were *him*, Christine. It were Adolf Hitler, I swear it was. I looked into his eyes up on that screen that evening in the cinema, and they was the same eyes. That Hitler, he don't look at you like other people do. He looks right through you, and that Fritz soldier was just the same. I never forgot his eyes. It was him, no mistake. D'you know what that means, Christine? I could've shot him there and then, done for him once and for all, and now that man is going to drag us all into another war. You listen to him. I know he is.'

"Christine did what she could to talk him round. It could have been someone else, she told him. Maybe it just looked like him. It was a long time ago. Memory plays tricks on you. You mustn't think such things, you'll make yourself ill. And anyway, maybe there won't be another war, you don't know. No one does.

"In the weeks that followed, Billy tried his level best to make himself believe her. He so wanted to, more than anything else in the world. He tried all he could to get the whole idea out of his mind altogether. But he couldn't. That newsreel in the cinema kept playing itself over and over inside his head. Every time he heard that voice on the radio, every time he watched a newsreel, it only made him surer that he had to be right. Every time he saw a photo in the newspaper he would look into those eyes and he would know there could be no mistake. No matter how often Christine tried to argue him round, how often she told him it couldn't be true, he knew it was, and insisted it was. In the end she could see there was no changing his mind.

"But even if it was true, she'd tell him then, it wouldn't be his fault, because he had only done what he thought was the right thing at the time; to be merciful was good, surely, even toward an enemy. And anyway, how could he have known that the soldier he had spared would turn out to be a monster? But nothing she said could make him feel better about what he had done. Billy clung to the one faint hope still left to him, that the Fritz soldier might just possibly have been someone else—small, black-haired, with a strange way of brushing his hair off his forehead, with dark staring eyes, but someone else. Just maybe, maybe, he kept telling himself, Christine could be right. His memory might be playing tricks on him. After all, it was, as she had so often reminded him, a very long time ago now.

"But then even that last faint glimmer of hope was taken away from him. Billy went one morning to the library to take some books back, and he happened to notice the title of a book up there on a shelf as he walked by. *Adolf Hitler*, it was called.

"He took the book down and opened it. There were a few pages of photographs in the middle. Every one of them made his heart beat faster, and one of them in particular.

"It was a photo of a group of German soldiers in the war, all in their caps, posing for the camera, a brick wall behind, all unsmiling, all looking directly at the camera.

"Billy recognized Adolf Hitler at once, slightly apart from the others, at the back, the smallest of them.

"The Fritz soldier, the soldier whose life he had saved. Below was his name. Corporal Adolf Hitler. No question now, no possible doubt about it. It was him."

PART FOUR

AN EAGLE IN THE SNOW

10

"ON THE WAY BACK HOME FROM THE LIBRARY, book in hand, Billy passed by the newspaper stand outside the station. The newspaper boy was shouting out the headlines. 'Hitler marches into Austria! Hitler invades Austria!'

"Billy stood there in the street, knowing for sure now that he was responsible for this, and for whatever Adolf Hitler had done or might do in the future. He could have stopped him twenty years before at the Battle of Marcoing, and he hadn't. He knew, as many others did too by now, that sooner or later Hitler would turn his attention to Britain, that it was only a matter of time."

"And he was right enough there, wasn't he?" Ma spoke suddenly, interrupting him out of the darkness. I thought she'd been asleep again, but I was wrong. "I mean, just think of it," she went on. "If that friend of yours, that Billy— Billy Byron was his name, right?—if he had pulled his trigger that day, then maybe we wouldn't be at war now, and Barney's dad wouldn't be fighting in the desert, and Dunkirk wouldn't have happened, nor the Blitz in London, or Coventry. All those people dead. It's all down to him. To lousy bleeding Adolf. We'd still have our home. Grandpa would still have his beloved horse, his Big Black Jack. One bullet, that's all it would have taken, one bullet, and none of this would have happened, would it? This story, hope you don't mind my asking—don't want to be rude or nothing—but you sure it's true? Don't sound very likely, if you ask me. You couldn't strike another match, could you? Can't seem to find my knitting needle." She was fumbling around on the seat beside me looking for it. "When is this train going to move?" she said.

I could hear the matchbox opening. The stranger was trying to light one, but it just sparked and died. "No good. Must have got damp," he said. "Usually reliable these matches are. Not to worry." But I was worried. "Here goes." He struck it again, again, and to my great relief, the match flared and lit up. Ma found her knitting needle almost at once—it had slipped down in between the seats.

I relished every moment that match lasted, and dreaded it going out. One more match left. I needed the story to stop me thinking about that. The match was already burning down fast.

"Is it true, really true, all of it?" I asked him. "What happened? What happened next?"

"All true enough, son. Wish it wasn't," said the stranger quietly. "It was like a curse on Billy's life, hung heavy over him every moment of every day after that. He never told anyone else about it, except Christine. Everyone, all his friends at work, knew he wasn't quite himself, could tell that he was sad deep inside, that he had troubles. They knew he'd been in the war, of course, what he'd done, the things he must have seen. Some of them, most of them, had been there too, seen the same things, things they only wanted to forget."

He shook the match out. We were deep in darkness again, a darkness that was blacker than ever. But I made up my mind then that I mustn't worry about it, just to listen to the story, lose myself in it.

"Billy's pals in the factory, they understood," the stranger went on, "or they thought they did. Like Christine, they did their best to cheer him up. But mostly they just left him be. They knew it was best. He went off every morning to the car factory as he had always done, did his job, and came back home to Christine in the evenings, but all the time the thought of what he had done, or rather *not* done, never left his mind, not for a moment.

"He didn't speak any more about it, not even at home now, but kept it to himself, locked inside, as week by week, month by month the news in Europe got worse. What would Hitler do next? Where else was he going to invade? When would it be our turn? It was all anyone talked about these days. Everyone noticed the change in Billy. He seemed to live in a world of his own, distant from his workmates and friends, and distant too now even from Christine, unable anymore to joke about his 'glum time' as he had before. They stopped going to the pictures, hardly ever went out. He even stopped his drawing, never got out his sketchbooks, not once, which Christine knew was the worst sign of all. He loved to draw. But not anymore. For Billy every day now was 'glum time,' and he never seemed to be able to lift himself out of it.

"Christine never stopped trying. She just hoped that one day he would be able to leave his sadness behind and be the man she had once known again, the man she loved, the man she knew was still inside there, who had saved her life when she was little, and who she knew had only ever done what he thought was the right thing, and was now suffering for it.

"And then in September, 1938 it was, a couple of years ago now—it seems like yesterday—Mr. Chamberlain, the prime minister then, goes off to see Mr. Hitler up in his mountain home, the Berghof they call it, at a place called Berchtesgaden in the Bavarian Alps, and does his best to do a deal with him. You remember that? Well, as we all know now—and we should have known it at the time— you can't hardly do a deal with the devil, can you? So our Mr. Chamberlain comes back home a few days later smiling all over his face and waving his piece of paper, telling

the world that everything was going to be just tickety-
boo, that he'd sorted everything out with Mr. Hitler, and
that we'd all have 'peace in our time.' Some peace we've
had, right? We all wanted to believe it, of course we
did. But most of us didn't, and Billy Byron certainly
didn't."

"Well, I never believed that Mr. Chamberlain neither,"
said Ma vociferously. "And what's more, nor did Barney's
dad, nor his grandpa. If you ask me, he was soft in the head
believing Hitler like he did. But Grandpa always says you
can't go blaming Chamberlain, any more than you can
blame the poor old hen when the wicked old fox comes
a-skulking around the henhouse. Only way you can look
after the hens is to keep out the fox, or better still, go after
him and kill him. And that's what we got to do. That's what
Barney's dad's doing right now. He's going after him. We'll
soon sort out that foxy Mr. Hitler, won't we, Barney?"

"Well, it's funny you should say that," the stranger went
on, "because all this time that's just what Billy had in mind.
The more he thought about it—and he thought about little
else these days—the more he knew he had to put right what
he had done wrong all those years before. Trouble was, of

course, he didn't know what to do, or even if anything could be done. And always at the back of his mind, there was still this last hope, that he could be wrong about this whole thing, that the Fritz soldier whose life he had spared might just have looked like Hitler, and been someone else altogether.

"Then out of the blue comes this phone call, to the manager's office at the Standard Car Factory where he works. Billy is on a tea break at the time, just sitting on his own and minding his own business when Mr. Bennet, the manager, comes looking for him. All of a fluster he is. He tells Billy he's got to come right away to the phone, now, that it's a real emergency. So off Billy goes rushing up to the manager's office, thinking that maybe Christine's had an accident or she's ill and in hospital or something. So he's worried himself sick by the time he gets to the office and picks up the phone.

"He recognizes the voice on the phone at once. It's someone whose voice he knows, but he can't put a face or name to it, can't work out who it is at all.

"'William Byron? That you, Mr. Byron?' says the man at the other end of the line. 'I'm sorry to trouble you, but I have something I have to tell you.' And Billy's still trying to picture the face to go with the voice, and then the voice tells him, and he still can't quite believe it. 'This is the prime minister here, Mr. Byron. Mr. Chamberlain. I need to speak to you about a matter of some importance.'"

11

"BILLY WAS FINDING IT HARD TO BELIEVE IT WAS really the prime minister speaking to him. He didn't know what to say. He was still trying to find his voice.

" 'You may know by now, Mr. Byron,' the prime minister went on, 'that I have been visiting Mr. Hitler out in Germany recently, at his home in the mountains. While I was there he told me a remarkable story, which I believe to be true, and which I promised I would tell you upon my return, because it concerns you. He told me that toward the end of the last war his life had been spared by a Tommy, at the Battle of Marcoing, he said, in September 1918. It is a moment he has never forgotten. He later discovered, through a photograph in a newspaper, that the Tommy soldier responsible for this act of mercy was you, Mr. Byron. He recognized you from a photograph of you receiving your Victoria Cross from His Majesty the king. He showed me the photograph himself. He still has it. Then he took me into his study and showed me a painting he has on the wall. It is of you, Mr. Byron, carrying a wounded man into a field hospital on your back, painted I believe by some Italian artist—I forget his name. A fine painting it is too. Dated 1918. Now, it has since been confirmed to me that you did in fact carry a man into a field hospital just like that, and I am assured that what Mr. Hitler has told me is very likely to be true. You were at the Battle of Marcoing, were you not?'

" 'I was, sir,' Billy replied.

" 'It was when you won your VC. Am I right?'

" 'Yes, sir.'

" 'And am I correct in saying that you did indeed spare the life of a German soldier in this battle?'

" 'I did, sir,' said Billy.

" 'As I thought. Well, Mr. Hitler, the German chancellor, wants me to tell you how grateful he is to you, and to pass on his thanks and his best wishes. I have to say, Mr. Byron, that what you did that day back in 1918, that act of mercy, might very well have helped to keep the peace twenty years later. Speaking of what happened that day to him, of how you spared his life, put Mr. Hitler in a good humor. I am delighted to say that he spoke of you and of the British Army with admiration and respect, all of which greatly helped to bring our discussions to a closer understanding, and in the end, I believe, to a most successful conclusion. By this one act of human kindness, you may well have helped the cause of peace. Good-bye, Mr. Byron, and thank you.'

"That was it. He put the phone down.

"As you can imagine, Billy walked home from the factory that day in a daze, a spring in his step, cock-a-hoop with new hope. All right, so the Fritz soldier whose life he had saved had been Adolf Hitler, but maybe, after all, just maybe, it didn't matter. Perhaps he had done the right thing all those years before. And Hitler might not be the ogre that Billy and everyone else seemed to believe he was. The man did have a heart. Maybe there really might be 'peace in our time,' as Mr. Chamberlain had promised us, and if so, then he, Private Billy Byron, might even have helped to make it happen."

"Chamberlain really phoned him up?" Ma interrupted him. "Just like that? How d'you know that? How do you know it's true?"

"Because Billy told me himself," said the stranger. "All of it. And Billy don't lie. Like I say, I know him, I've knowed him just about all my life. He keeps a lot to himself, but he don't lie. He don't make stuff up. He's not like that."

"Is that the end of the story?" I asked him then. To be honest, I was disappointed. I wasn't that bothered if the tale was true or not. I liked exciting endings, and to end on a phone call wasn't exactly exciting, no matter who it came from, whether it was a prime minister or not.

But more important, I remembered then that there was only one more match left, and the train was still stuck in the blackness of the tunnel. I needed the story to go on, to be longer. I needed something to take my mind off the darkness.

"No, it's not the end," the stranger replied. "But that would have been the best ending, son, wouldn't it? The happy-ever-after ending. Peace in our time. No more war. That was the ending Billy wanted, the ending we all wanted. I wish I could make it a happy ending for you. But one way or another, things didn't quite work out like that, as you know. They often don't. Otherwise Coventry wouldn't have been blitzed, and your house would still be standing, and you and I wouldn't be here, and I wouldn't be telling you this story. The ending may not be the ending you want, son, but I can promise you one thing: it won't be the ending you expect."

He paused for a while before he went on. "Anyway," he began again, "it looked like things *would* work out, for a while at least. Billy was almost his old self after that phone call. He began drawing once more—birds mostly, in particular a woodpecker that came again and again to the garden, black and white he was, with a flash of bright red behind. Christine was overjoyed at the change in him. She had her Billy back.

"They started going out to the pictures again. But the trouble was that every time they went, there was another of those newsreels to sit through, and every time they showed soldiers on the march, German soldiers, thousands of them, and Hitler was up there on the screen and he wasn't talking peace. Still, despite that, Billy went on hoping for the best. S'pose we all did. But then—when was it?—in March last year, 1939, Hitler marches his soldiers into Czechoslovakia, occupies the whole country, and Billy knows then what we all knew, that his jack-booted army wouldn't stop at Czechoslovakia. We all realized now, and Billy did too, that the piece of paper that Chamberlain waved in the air that day was worthless. We'd all been fooled. We'd all believed what we wanted to believe, what Hitler wanted us to believe. But after the invasion of Czechoslovakia we all knew the truth. We all knew what was coming. It wasn't a case anymore of *if* there was a war, it was *when*.

"Time and again Billy and Christine saw him on the newsreels in the cinema, Hitler shaking his fist at the world, Hitler swaggering, hectoring, bullying, threatening. Billy saw the endless parades of strutting, goose-stepping soldiers, of tanks rolling by, the skies full of warplanes, and always Hitler was standing there, reveling in his power, and hungry for more. Billy knew for sure what we all know now: that here was a tyrant, a man of evil, who had only one thing in mind—to make war, to conquer and destroy.

"All Billy could think now was that somehow this man had to be stopped; that twenty years before he had done the wrong thing and now he must do the right thing. He had to right the wrong he had done. He decided once and for all what he was going to do. He thought of the thousands, and millions maybe, of little Christines out there. It would be just like it had been before in the last war. He had to stop the suffering before it began, that was all there was to it. He had no choice.

"Billy went alone, never said a word to Christine. He just walked out of the house early one morning as if he was going to work. But he didn't have lunch in his bag. He had other things. He had his passport and papers, some money, and hidden away in the false bottom of the suitcase, the pistol from the biscuit tin under the bed. In his jacket pocket he had his lucky black pebble from Bridlington. He had his box of pencils and his sketchbook too, and his little folding stool strapped to his suitcase. He had everything he needed.

"They were all part of the plan. He had thought it through, down to the last detail. Billy knew he would need all the luck he could get for the plan to work. He'd left a note on the mantelpiece, telling Christine that he had something he had to do, something that wouldn't wait, that he would be back in a couple of weeks or so. In the note he asked her to go to the factory to tell Mr. Bennet that he'd be off work for a while, to tell him it was his gammy leg giving him trouble again, to tell him he was sorry. She wasn't to worry, he wrote. He'd be back, and he loved her. He always had done, and he always would."

12

"BILLY GOT ON THE TRAIN IN COVENTRY THAT morning, knowing exactly what he was intending to do. He had found out all he could from the library, from the newspapers. He knew where he was going. That had been simple enough to work out. He had decided that near Hitler's mountain home in the Alps, the Berghof, near Berchtesgaden, where Mr. Chamberlain had gone before, would be the best place to do it—he'd seen photographs of that place and of Hitler walking his dog in the snow, with the mountains and the forests behind. He had read that Hitler went there as often as he could. But exactly how it was to be done, where and when—he knew that would depend on keeping to his plan, on fate, and on his own patience. He only knew it had to be done, had to be tried, whatever the consequences.

"So he took the train to London, and then the boat across the Channel to Calais. He didn't doubt for one moment as he was leaving that this was the only thing he could do, but as he looked out from the stern of the ship at the white cliffs of Dover, he wondered if he would ever see them again. It wasn't likely, he thought. In his mind it was as if he was going over the top again, just gritting his teeth and doing what had to be done. He knew then that the chances of survival were not good. *What will be, will be*, he thought. It helped, in a way, that he began to feel seasick then—he had forgotten how that felt after all these years. His stomach churned with the roll of the ship. How he wished he had stayed at home. The sight of the French coast lifted his spirits, but the waves kept heaving until they were in port.

"The French customs official hardly gave him or his passport a glance, and soon he was in Paris, and on the train down to Munich. At the German frontier in the middle of the night it was a very different matter altogether. Everyone in the carriage was questioned by a frontier policeman, passports and papers scrupulously examined. He seemed courteous enough with his questions. But Billy felt the threat behind every one.

" 'And why are you coming to Germany, please? What reason?'

" 'I'm an artist,' Billy told him. 'I am going walking in the Alps, drawing the mountains, the wildlife, the birds.'

"The policeman demanded to see his work.

"Billy showed him his sketchbook.

"He seemed satisfied, impressed even. 'Good,' he said, 'very good. You will like our mountains. They are very beautiful, the most beautiful in the world. And now your suitcase, please? I have to see your suitcase.'

"Billy opened it for him, his heart pounding in his ears.

"The policeman picked up the pencil case first and opened it. Then he took out his pajamas, and his socks, all his clothes, examining them all closely. He pulled out everything, emptied the suitcase entirely, then felt around the bottom of it, the false bottom, with the pistol hidden and taped underneath it, right under his searching fingers.

"Time itself seemed to slow during those moments, so

that the moments became minutes. At last, he seemed sat-isfied. 'You travel with very little,' said the frontier police-man. 'Welcome to Germany. Heil Hitler!'

"And that was it. Billy could breathe again.

"Munich station was full of soldiers, full of policemen. So many people seemed to be in uniform, even some of the children too. There were swastikas everywhere, worn as armbands, hanging on buildings. A military band was playing somewhere, the thumping of drums and clashing of cymbals echoing around the station—drums of war, Billy felt. The more he looked about him, the more he could see that this was a country making ready for war, on the march. It only confirmed in him his determination to go through with what he had in mind.

"He didn't stay in Munich any longer than he had to. He could feel there were watching eyes everywhere. From Munich he caught a bus to the mountains. He rented a room in a quiet village he had found on the map, just a few miles from Hitler's house in the mountains—far enough away, he hoped, not to arouse suspicion. The important thing, Billy knew, was to be inconspicuous, which was not easy. He was obviously foreign, obviously English, and a tourist. So to begin with, he played the part he needed to play, going nowhere near the Berghof, just going out walking every day, sitting down on his stool and sketching somewhere near the village, till everyone got used to seeing him about, seeing him intent on his drawing.

"Even in the evenings he would be working away at his sketchbook in the village café, puffing on his pipe, drinking his beer. His sketchbook was full of drawings of the mountains, of the villagers, of the snow-covered houses, of the church, of the deer he had seen, the hares, the eagles. The local people were friendly enough—some of them even gave him a drink from time to time. They seemed intrigued by his drawings—even the village policeman. They were obviously delighted when they recognized this house or that, particularly if it was their own house; or this villager or that, especially when it was themselves or one of the family. Many of them were openly admiring of his work, and would try out their broken English on him. But always from the wall of the café the picture of Adolf Hitler looked down on him. Every time Billy looked up at it—and he tried not to—he felt recognition passing between them.

"Every day now Billy would go out walking farther

in the snow, every day a little closer to the Berghof, but still always, if anyone saw him, he'd be sitting there on his stool in the snow and drawing. There were often eagles wheeling about the sky, their cries shrill and clear on the air, so he always had something to draw, and something to show the villagers in the evening on his return.

"But now as he looked and drew, he was also searching out the best place to do what he had come to do, spending long cold hours on the edge of the forest, a mile or so across the valley from the Berghof, perched there high on the side of the hill. The house was bigger, grander, more imposing than Billy had imagined from the photographs he had seen of it. And there were more guards too, in black uniforms mostly. He saw all the comings and goings on the road—the cars, the trucks, the soldiers. But of Hitler himself there was no sign. If he was there, he was not going out for his walks.

"All the time, as Billy was watching the eagles and drawing them, he was asking himself how he would do it when the time came, and wondering how long he would have to wait, whether Hitler would ever come. Every evening as he sat there sketching in the bar he would be eavesdropping, listening for any mention of the *Führer*. He understood a little German—from prisoners in the last war—not much, but enough to get the gist of things, enough to say thank you and please, *danke, bitte, bitte schön.* There were often mentions of Adolf Hitler—he was much talked about.

"Then one evening, after a week or so, it seemed as if everyone in the village café was talking about '*der Führer.*' They were pointing to his picture on the wall, trying to tell Billy. There was high excitement in their voices, a new excitement. Something was up. He was there, Billy was sure of it. The man he had been waiting for had arrived. His moment had come. It was time."

13

"SO FOR THE FIRST TIME THE NEXT DAY, WHEN HE
went out walking, Billy took his sketchbook and his
stool as usual, but he also took the pistol with him inside
his jacket. He waited for hours hidden in the trees, longing
for Hitler to take his walk, willing him to do it.

"He didn't come. All that came were the clouds, rolling up the valley, giant clouds that soon shrouded the trees,
the house, the mountains.

"Day after day, Billy waited. Hitler never came. But despite how thick the clouds, how hard it snowed, or how
cold he was, he only became more determined to stick it

out, no matter what. He wasn't going to give up now. He never once in all this time doubted this was the right thing to do. He only doubted whether Hitler would come at all, whether he would ever have the opportunity to do what he had come for. He found if he concentrated hard on drawing the eagles, it helped pass the time, helped him forget the cold, helped soften the disappointment.

"Then one afternoon Hitler did come, and when he did, Billy wasn't ready for him.

"The eagle he had been drawing, which had been circling high over the peaks, went into a sudden stoop, swooping down, closer, closer, his talons open, ready for the kill. Billy hadn't even noticed the hare, until the eagle was on him, landing in the open snow, only yards away from the trees where Billy was sitting. He had never in his life been this close to an eagle, and once he had recovered from the surprise, he drew fast, not wanting to miss the moment.

"Then, somewhere, a dog started barking. The eagle lifted off, lumbering into the air, the hare limp in his talons. A dog was bounding down through the snow toward the eagle, toward Billy, hackles up. It was a huge Alsatian, his bark and his growl fearsome, intimidating.

"That was when Billy looked up and saw Hitler, in his peaked cap and his long black coat. He was still some way away. He was strolling down the road, and there were six or seven other men, all of them in black uniforms, two of them readying their rifles. Everything was happening so fast and not at all as Billy had expected it. But he kept his head. The dog would not stop him. The sight of the raised rifles would not stop him. He was going to do it. He had to. This was the opportunity he had been waiting for all this time.

"He stepped calmly out of the trees and stood there on the snow-covered hillside, his pistol held behind his back, ready. There he waited. At his feet there was a spattering of blood on the snow, where the eagle had made his kill. Hitler was still a hundred yards off, with his soldiers, some of them running now down the road toward Billy. Billy waited, waited. It had to be close, as close as possible. He must not miss.

"But the dog was coming closer all the while, barking wildly, snarling. Billy had waited too long.

"The dog was on him before he knew it, leaping up and knocking him to the ground.

"He was flat on his back in the snow, the dog astride him, not biting him at all, as Billy had expected, but licking his face all over. He still had the pistol in his hand. He gripped it. He could still do it, if only the dog would get off him. But the soldiers were already all around him. Too late, too late. At the last moment, he plunged the pistol into the snow, thrust it down deep, as deep as it would go. Then they were pulling the dog off him and hauling him roughly to his feet.

"Moments later, Adolf Hitler was standing there, right in front of him, looking him in the eye. Billy knew at once that Hitler recognized him. Neither spoke a word, but for a few moments both stood there, knowing one another, remembering. Billy could feel the hardness of his pistol in the snow under his foot.

"The two soldiers had Billy by the arms, gripping him tight. Hitler waved them away. Then he simply nodded, turned, and walked off. The dog was sniffing round Billy's feet, more interested now in the blood of the hare than anything else. Billy stayed where he was, the pistol under his foot, until they called the dog off. Then he found himself alone on the hillside, watching Hitler walk away, just as he had done twenty years before, and knowing in his heart of hearts as he stood there that he could no more have shot him this time than he had before."

The stranger paused then for a few moments and cleared his throat.

"Well, that's about it, almost," he went on. "Billy came home to Christine, and told no one, except her, where he had been nor what he had tried to do. She said he had tried to do the right thing, but that it would have been the wrong thing had he done it. And he knew she was right about that."

"So how do you know then if he didn't tell anyone except her?" I asked him.

"Ah, well, that'd be telling, wouldn't it?" he said mysteriously. "He's a sharp one, your boy, missus. Just like Billy. And you're a Mulberry Road lad just like we were. S'why I told you all about it, son. Like I said, no one else knows the story, just three of us, and Billy, of course. And he wouldn't mind you knowing. In fact, I reckon he'd want you to know. S'how we live on, in our stories, right?"

"All down to that ruddy dog," Ma said. "I can't believe it. If he hadn't knocked that Billy over, then Hitler might be dead and the whole war might never have happened. Never did like dogs, specially not Alsatians. They's wolves, more'n dogs."

"Let's all get a bit of shut-eye, shall we?" said the stranger in the darkness. "Only one more match left. Better not waste it, eh? Still, you'll manage without it now, I reckon. Be out of here soon enough."

"Good story, mister," I said. He never replied. We went to sleep then, all of us. I don't know for how long.

The train jolted us awake, and a moment or two later it was on the move. Then we were out of the tunnel altogether, the train driver taking it slowly, I thought, just in case, and I was peering up out of the window looking to see if there were any more fighters up there. There weren't. The clouds were gone too. It was a clear blue sky.

Then Ma said suddenly: "Where's he gone then?"

The stranger wasn't there. There was no one in the seat opposite. Ma and I looked at one another. "Must've gone to the lav," she said. But the stranger never came back. A minute or so after this, the guard opened the carriage door.

"Going to be a little late into London," he said. "You all right in here?"

"That man that was in here with us," Ma said. "You seen him?"

"What man?" said the guard. "There was just the two of you when I came in before. Weren't no man."

I remembered the hat then that the stranger had put up in the luggage rack by our case. I looked up. It wasn't there.

"He was here," Ma insisted. "He was, wasn't he, Barney?"

"Course," I said. "Course he was."

The guard raised his eyebrows at us as if we were mad. "If you say so, madam, if you say so. Now if you don't mind, I've got a job to do." And he went out, sliding the door closed behind him.

Ma and I looked at one another. "He told us that story, didn't he?" I began. "About Hitler, about Billy not killing him in the war when he could have, when he should have, and then about going over to Germany with his pistol to shoot him in the mountains, and the eagle and all that. He told us, didn't he? Weren't just a dream, were it, Ma?"

Ma reached down then and picked up something lying at her feet. It was the box of Swan Vestas matches. She opened it. Inside were four used matches, one still un-used, and that wasn't all. There was a small black pebble and a spent cartridge. She struck the match. "Real matches," she said. "Everything was real. No dream, Barney. No dream."

EPILOGUE

MA AND I COULD TALK OF NOTHING ELSE ALL
the way to London, then all the way to Cornwall. It
really was as if we had both dreamed the same dream, every
last detail of it. But we knew, both of us, that it hadn't been
a dream at all, that it couldn't have been. We had the evi-
dence in the Swan Vestas matchbox.

When we arrived in Mevagissey late that night, we
had to tell Aunty Mavis at once all about the stranger on
the train and the amazing story he had told us. We just
had to tell someone. We showed her the matchbox, showed
her the lucky black pebble from Bridlington and the spent
cartridge. Aunty Mavis was never the best of listeners, but

she listened right through to the very end, her eyes growing wider and wider.

When we had finished she said nothing; she just got up and went to the kitchen dresser. She brought back a newspaper and smoothed it out on the table in front of us. "This morning's paper," she said. "Look."

The headline read: "First World War hero dies in Coventry Blitz." And there was the face of the stranger in the train, staring up at us out of the photograph underneath.

Ma read it out, her voice a whisper. "William (Billy) Byron, VC, MM, DCM, one of the most decorated Private soldiers of the Great War, was amongst those killed in the recent *Luftwaffe* blitz on Coventry. His wife, Christine, a teacher in a local council school, was also killed. Mr. Byron, who was serving in the Civil Defense Force, having been out on duty all night and day, rescuing people from the remnants of their homes, came home to find his own house destroyed. He was killed by falling masonry whilst trying to find his wife in the ruins of their house. Mr. Byron worked at the Standard Car Factory in Coventry. He was forty-five years of age."

AFTERWORD

HENRY TANDEY IS, RIGHTLY, REMEMBERED AS an exceptional soldier of the First World War. But his heroism is embroidered by a story that, if true, is one of the great "what if" events of history—moments in time so pivotal that one different decision forever changes the course of history.

Henry, born in 1891, was the son of a stonemason and a laundress. The family appears to have fallen on hard times after Henry's father, James, quarreled with his own prosperous father. James is said to have had an evil temper, perhaps influenced by drink. We know Henry spent some time in an orphanage, but we do not know why.

As an adult Henry was only eight and a half stone and five feet five inches tall. He joined the army in 1910, perhaps to escape his family situation, or the backbreaking, tedious work of a boiler stoker in a Leamington hotel, or perhaps inspired by a sense of adventure. We do not know because Henry kept no diary. If he wrote letters home, none of them survived. Our knowledge of him comes from newspaper interviews, dispatches, and his medal record.

Nicknamed "Napper," he was initially a private in the Green Howards regiment, which fought in the Battle of Ypres in October 1914. When the regiment was relieved

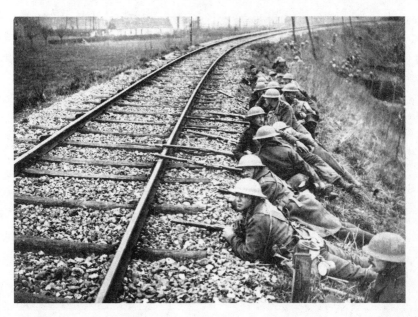

on October 20, seven hundred of one thousand men were dead or badly injured. Meanwhile Henry had rescued some wounded from buildings under shellfire, commenting only: "We were lucky. We managed to get all the wounded back without a casualty."

By late summer 1918 Henry had been wounded three times and mentioned in army dispatches. Then, in an unparalleled burst of heroics by a single soldier, Henry Tandey won the three highest awards for bravery in separate actions in a six-week period.

First he received the Distinguished Conduct Medal. He had been in charge of a reserve bombing party. When

soldiers in front of him were held up by German fire, he led two volunteers across open ground to the rear of the enemy. They rushed a machine-gun post and took twenty prisoners. Next he earned the Military Medal for "exhibiting great heroism and devotion to duty." He "went out under most heavy shellfire and carried back a badly wounded man on his back" and saved three others. The next day he volunteered to lead an attack on a trench.

A German officer "shot at him at point-blank and missed. Private Tandey, quite regardless of danger" drove the enemy away.

On September 28, 1918, Henry earned the highest British military decoration awarded for valor "in the face of the enemy"—the Victoria Cross. Nearly nine million British and Commonwealth people served at some stage in the First World War. Only 628 VCs were awarded, mainly to officers. His platoon came under machine-gun attack when attempting to cross a wooden bridge over a canal.

Henry crawled forward, replaced broken planks under fire, and led the way across to silence the gun. Later, surrounded and outnumbered, he led eight men in a bayonet charge, driving thirty-seven Germans into the hands of other British troops.

He had earned his three gallantry awards with his new battalion in the Duke of Wellington's regiment. One senior officer wryly told Henry that his bravery could not adequately be rewarded because he had already won all the gallantry medals available!

After the war Henry stayed on in the army. The only thing of note we know of his postwar service is that he was promoted to acting lance corporal, but reverted to private within a year at his own request. We don't know why.

In 1926 he moved back to Leamington, living an undistinguished civilian life. For the next thirty-eight years he was Commissionaire at the Standard Motor Company. But during the Second World War he acted as a part-time recruiting officer for the army and as a fire warden in Coventry. He married but had no children. He died in December 1977.

Did Henry Tandey have the wounded Adolf Hitler in his rifle sights on the Western Front in the First World War? We will never know for sure. Henry recalled: "I took aim but couldn't shoot a wounded man, so I let him go."

Hitler is known to have owned a copy of a painting by Fortunino Matania, commissioned by the Green Howards in 1923. Henry appears in it with an injured comrade over his shoulder.

In 1938 Hitler told British prime minister Neville Chamberlain why he had the picture depicting Henry: "That man came so near to killing me that I thought I should never see Germany again. Providence saved me from such devilishly accurate fire as those boys were aiming at us." Hitler asked Chamberlain to convey his thanks to Henry. Henry's reaction was: "According to them, I've met Adolf Hitler. Maybe they're right, but I can't remember him."

In 1940, after the Germans firebombed Coventry, Henry worked to rescue people from the rubble. He was quoted in the press: "I didn't like to shoot a wounded

man, but if I'd known who this corporal would turn out to be, I'd give ten years now to have five minutes' clairvoyance then."

Some have questioned whether Hitler would really recognize his "savior," probably mud-spattered, from a distance. Is it credible that he would remember his face twenty years later? But if a British Tommy did spare Hitler's life when he lay wounded, who better, from Hitler's point of view, to be fate's instrument than the most decorated British private?

The story has been repeated as truth, and denied as often, but Private Henry Tandey will forever be linked with the tag "the soldier who didn't shoot Hitler."

Thank you for reading this FEIWEL AND FRIENDS book.
The Friends who made

AN EAGLE
IN THE SNOW

possible are:

JEAN FEIWEL, *Publisher*

LIZ SZABLA, *Editor in Chief*

RICH DEAS, *Senior Creative Director*

ALEXEI ESIKOFF, *Senior Managing Editor*

RAYMOND ERNESTO COLÓN, *Senior Production Manager*

ANNA ROBERTO, *Editor*

HOLLY WEST, *Editor*

CHRISTINE BARCELLONA, *Associate Editor*

EMILY SETTLE, *Administrative Assistant*

ANNA POON, *Editorial Assistant*

Follow us on Facebook or visit us online at mackids.com.
OUR BOOKS ARE FRIENDS FOR LIFE.